TALLULAH'S TEMPTATION

SEA SHENANIGANS, BOOK 1

ROBYN PETERMAN

WWW.ROBYNPETERMAN.COM

ACKNOWLEDGMENTS

Starting a new series is delightfully frightening. I love everything about it! LOL And I can't wait for you guys to read this book. I laughed so hard while writing it it's embarrassing.

Pirate Doug and the gang are now some of my favorite people.

Anyhoo, as always, I write the book, but it takes a whole lot of wonderful people to make the magic happen. I am a lucky girl because I have a whole lot of wonderful people in my life.

Renee George, thank you for my beautiful cover. You are the bomb!

Meg Weglartz, thank you. You are the best editor a gal could have!

Donna McDonald, thank you. You are the most brilliant MST partner in the world!

My beta readers—Wanda and Susan, thank you. I adore you.

Steve, Henry and Audrey, thank you. You make everything worth it.

And to my readers... thank you. I do this for you.

For Renee.
You are my Cookie and you make beautiful covers!
YOU ROCK!

BOOK DESCRIPTION

Pirate Doug

What in the Chicken of the Sea was I thinking to agree to this half arsed Otherworld Defense Agency mission?

I'm the most absurdly good looking Vampire Pirate of the High Seas. Being on the run for my life is very important work... and a freaking full time job. Defending Mermaids from some vicious Sea Hags is going to cut into my pilfering time.

Unacceptable.

Even though this is a very *bad* move on my part, I know I'll eventually agree—too many bounties on my arse to refuse, and the thought of a certain Mermaid makes my roger quite jolly.

However, Tallulah, the leader of the Mystical Isle Pod of Mermaids, isn't going to be happy to see me... at all. The horrible, sexy, breathtaking woman has been starring in my dreams for too many years to count. Sadly, just when my mind wanders to the really *good nookie part,* the dream ends with her lopping my Johnson off.

I just hope to Hell and back that the Sea Hags have some outstanding booty to steal. If I'm going to have to regrow my tallywhacker, the treasure had better damned well be worth it.

Tallulah

Running a tourist trap for humans in the Bermuda Triangle had sounded like a fine plan—until it wasn't.

With the Sea Hags gunning for our island and ruining our questionably successful business, I did what any desperate Mermaid would do. I called for backup.

Of course, getting help from the Otherworld Defense Agency is risky as they don't usually deal with ocean creatures. Whatever. Desperate times call for crappy measures. Chances are they'll send freaking Pirates. I hate Pirates…

Well, I hate one Pirate in particular.

Hopefully, it won't be the one seafaring jackhole I despise more than any other. Pirate Doug would be an idiot to show his face here after what he'd done. Not only did the dumbass abscond with our treasure, the son-of-a-bitch took my heart with him as well.

I'll tear his sorry ass to shreds if he so much as steps even one hairy toe on my island.

PIRATE DOUG

"DOUG, THIS IS AN OFFER YOU WOULD BE FOOLISH TO REFUSE," Renee said, running a hand through her curly red hair in frustration.

"*Pirate* Doug," I reminded her for the fourth time. If the human woman—as attractive and beddable as she was—couldn't be bothered to remember my title, I couldn't be bothered to listen.

I was an extremely busy Vampire Pirate of the High Seas. Being on the run for my life was a full fucking time job. Sitting still in an office on dry land was making me itchy. I was a sitting duck for my inordinately long list of enemies.

Of course killing me was an almost impossible feat, but I could be dismembered quite easily by the right foe. My arms and legs would regenerate, but it really pissed me off to have to regrow the appendages—not to mention dry socket sucked.

I'd had the same legs for three hundred years and I planned on keeping it that way. Now my arms were an entirely different story. Taking a week off to sprout new limbs was a dangerous proposition for someone as *in demand* as I was.

"So let me get this straight," I said, casing the office for something to abscond with. Sadly, there was nothing shiny in sight. Either Renee had hidden all her precious booty or she didn't have any. "You're going to pay off my debts if I agree to take this appalling offer I have yet to hear?"

"No," she said with a barely disguised eye roll. "No one in their right mind would pay off your astronomical and wildly illegal financial woes."

"So then I'm wasting my time and risking my life by being here," I said, standing up to take my leave.

"Sit," Renee commanded in a voice that made me a bit randy and resulted in my breeches growing tight.

The small woman had large balls. I found her rudeness wildly arousing. Not that I would make a play for the owner of the Otherworld Defense Agency. She was mated to two Werewolves. Those hairy bastards were vicious. Besides, I preferred nonhuman women who enjoyed the sea—much more durable in the boudoir on my ship.

"Your debt is insurmountable," she pointed out.

"Thank you," I replied with a gallant bow.

"That wasn't a compliment," she said, biting back a grin.

"My bad," I said with my most charming smile.

I was obnoxiously aware that I was an obscenely good looking bastard. It had come in handy over my many centuries. Pretty people could get away with murder—not that I was into that sort of thing. I was far more into priceless objects, rare artifacts and getting laid on a very regular basis. Murder only came into play when someone was gunning for my sexy ass.

"Doug," she began.

"*Pirate* Doug."

"Right. *Pirate Doug*," Renee amended with a shake of her head and a chuckle. "I can have the most egregious bounty removed from your idiot head if you take the job."

"You can get the Gnomes off my arse?" I inquired,

surprised. I let the *idiot* comment go mostly because it was accurate and the rest of her statement was very intriguing.

Gnomes were the bane of my fabulous existence at the moment. The bald bastards were after me for too many reasons to count. Of course bedding the gal pal of their head honcho a decade ago didn't help, but draining their international bank accounts was certainly high on their list of my transgressions as well.

"They owe us a favor or seven," she said cryptically. "We can erase what you've done. However, I'd like to suggest that you steer clear of the Gnomes in the future."

"Could you be more specific?" I inquired. Implied rules and vague hints were not my forte.

"Sure," she replied with a sigh and then a laugh. "Keep your dick in your pants and stop stealing their shit. Period. We can't negate your future crimes—only the ones you've already committed."

"Interesting," I said, running my hand over my well-trimmed goatee and considering this offer although I still had no idea what I had to do. I was tempted to say yes even though the mission was a mystery. I'd had far too many close calls of late. It was getting quite tiresome to have to fight off those bloodthirsty Gnome sons of bitches.

There were plenty of people and species to steal from. I could avoid looting the Gnomes for a few hundred years. However, keeping my man tool in my breeches might prove to be difficult. The female Gnomes adored me. They were animals in the sack and delightfully violent—all attributes that made my roger quite jolly. Although, living to see tomorrow did appeal…

"Let's say… *hypocritically*, I accept your offer. What exactly did you have in mind?" I asked, sitting back down, but rearranging my chair so I could see the exit clearly. Never good to let someone sneak up from behind. That's how I'd lost my left arm three months ago.

"I'm sorry, what did you just say?" Renee asked, seemingly confused. "Do you mean hypothetically?"

I paused in thought. I had been told it made me look smarter...

"No. I'm fairly sure I'm a hypocrite. Did I use it in the sentence wrong? I have a word of the day calendar and I've been trying to stretch the old vocabulary. I've found pretending to have a higher IQ gets me laid more regularly."

The human woman was stunned to silence for a brief moment and then had an alarming coughing fit that caused her face to turn a bright red—or possibly she was choking to death. No matter. She was clearly bowled over by my brains and brawn. I was gorgeous and had a legendary trouser snake. However, if she keeled over in my presence I'd have to answer to the fucking Werewolves. That was not my idea of a good time.

"Do you need me to hemlock you?" I inquired politely.

Her eyes grew wide and I wondered if she was daft. I'd heard quite the opposite, but her behavior was strange.

"Umm... no," she said, getting control of herself with effort. "That won't be necessary."

"Very well then," I replied. "What are the terms?"

"You still have your ship?" she asked, wiping a few tears from her eyes as she cleared her throat several times.

"I have a fleet," I replied proudly.

"Do I want to know how you amassed a fleet?"

I paused and winked at the harried woman. "Probably not."

"Fine," Renee said, scrubbing her hand over her mouth to hide her grin. "We've received a distress call from a Mermaid pod in the Bermuda Triangle. They're being attacked by Sea Hags."

I froze for a brief moment. Mermaids were my weakness—

well, one Mermaid in particular, but she wanted to off my fine ass. Whatever, I didn't need that delectable swimming hooker. She'd had her chance. It was completely irrelevant that *I'd* fucked it up.

"And this is a problem?" I asked, not clear on why anyone would want to save either of those species.

"*Yes*, it's a problem," Renee said. "Mermaids are good and Sea Hags are not."

"Not sure where you're getting your Intel, but the last Mermaid I encountered tried to castrate me. Do you have any clue how long it takes to grow back a schlong?"

Again the poor human was rendered mute. I really didn't know how she ran a business if she couldn't hold a decent conversation.

"Well, do you?" I demanded.

"No," she choked out and then narrowed her eyes. "And I can live out the rest of my life without knowing. The mission is to help the Mermaids fight off the Sea Hags. While your intellect is debatable, your skills are unrivaled. This is why I'm offering you the mission. If you can't do it, fine. We're done here."

Renee stood up and offered me her hand. This was not going my way. I hated when things didn't go my way. I usually threw an epic fit, but somehow didn't think that would go over too well right now. And I wasn't quite sure if she'd just insulted me.

What I *needed* was to get the fucking Gnomes off my arse. So what if I had to help some legless wenches. If I wore a protective codpiece over my Johnson, I would probably be fine. As long as it wasn't the Mystical Isle Pod... I'd be a dead Pirate walking with those waterlogged, sexy freaks of nature.

"Wait," I said, ignoring her outstretched hand. "So what you're saying is that I need to send the Sea Hags to Davy Jones' locker—or at least make a few Black Spots to scare the heinous scallywags off the water loving, scaly tailed bitches' arses? However, I'd like to know if hornswoggling is off the table, from what I understand the Sea Hags have impressive booty."

"Umm... I think so," Renee said, trying to decipher my statement. "If that means you'll stop the Sea Hags from killing the Mermaids and stealing their land—then yes. Pretty sure you don't think the Hags have nice asses, so I'll assume you're inquiring if you can loot their treasures?"

I always forgot that most didn't speak Pirate. However, the human woman was right on the money.

"Yes," I replied with a grin.

She shook her head and closed her eyes. "If you steal from the Sea Hags, I don't want to know about it. However, there will be no stealing from the Mermaids."

"Deal," I said, taking her small hand in mine and shaking it. "Piece of cake. And what is the pod of man-eating Mermaids called?"

There were hundreds of those tail wagging swimming hookers in the Bermuda Triangle. There was no way in Hell it could be the one pod that wanted me strung up and beheaded.

"It's the Mystical Isle Pod. Do you know of them?"

It was now my turn to be speechless. The prospect of seeing the one that got away—or rather, the one who tried to castrate me for a slight misunderstanding—was horrifyingly tempting. If I declined the job on the outside chance that I would lose my pecker, I'd have to deal with the Gnomes. The Gnomes could mean actual death for me. Weighing the cost of my dong against the cost of my life took me a few minutes.

I smiled at Renee so she wouldn't be alerted to my inner terror and turmoil. Deciding to risk my wanker as opposed to my life, I nodded and widened my smile. I prayed to Poseidon that it didn't resemble a constipated wince.

"I do know of them," I replied, nodding slowly and slightly bent at the waist already in mourning for my nads. "Haven't seen those gals in a century. It shall be jolly to get reacquainted."

"Are you sure?" she asked, eyeing me strangely.

"Positive," I answered. "Absolutely positive."

Positive that this was a very *bad* move on my part. Tallulah, the leader of the vicious Mystical Isle Pod of Mermaids, wasn't exactly fond of me... and that was putting it mildly. The horrible, sexy, breathtaking woman had been starring in my dreams for too many years to count. Sadly, just when my mind wandered to the really *good nookie part*, the dream ended with her whacking my Johnson off. I just hoped to Hell and back that the Sea Hags had some outstanding booty. If I was going to have to regrow my tallywhacker, the treasure had better damn well be good.

2

TALLULAH

"TO YOUR LEFT," I SHOUTED TO ARIEL AS I DUCKED A BLAST OF salty magic aimed at my head.

"Ask any tuna you happen to see," Ariel grunted as she slapped the head off one of the more aggressive Sea Hags with her tail. "Who's the best mermaid? That would be ME!"

There was no time to groan and close my eyes at Ariel's terrible ode to the tuna fish song. I'd nail her for that shortly— as long as I lived through the next few minutes. At least she hadn't burst into *Part of Your World*.

"Throw a glitter fish bomb," Madison yelled as she wrestled with a deadly Hag, squeezing so hard that the Hag popped like a green goop-filled balloon.

Well, that was certainly one way to eliminate the enemy...

"No can do," I yelled back. "We have human paying guests on the island. Can't risk them. It's hand to hand, ladies."

"But wait," Ariel said as she expertly twisted a Sea Hag in a knot. "I thought the humans already paid in full."

"They did," I replied, tossing a bolt of magic at a trio of Hags who were trying to behead me.

"Then what's the problem?" Ariel questioned, avoiding a Hag dagger that had been lobbed at her.

"Not following," I called out as I took out a few more with my tail.

"If they've already paid, why do we care if they die? There are kajillions of humans."

"I'm going to pretend I didn't hear that—and kajillions is *not* a word," I snapped and shook my head in disgust. "We can't become the island known for randomly killing humans. First off, it's wrong… and secondly, it will ruin our business."

"Well, crap," Misty complained, hurling a stinky Sea Hag over her head at the others still gunning for her. "Goddess, their breath smells so bad their toothbrushes must pray at night."

"Or else their teeth try to escape," Madison said, landing an excellent left hook to the face of a Hag that was trying to drown her. "Oh, wait," she added with a laugh as she popped up from beneath a wave and sent a sizzling shot of magic right at the Hag. "They don't have teeth. My bad."

The normally teal blue sea was awash with blood—theirs and ours. This was the fifth attack in as many days by the heinous Sea Hags. I wasn't sure how much longer we could take the assaults and come out on top, but my sister Mermaids and I wouldn't go down without one hell of a fight.

The day had dawned bright and sunny—it had been perfect. Now? Not so much. Normally our island was a peaceful paradise, albeit a bit dated. But this morning the lovely scenery was being polluted by vicious, horrifying Sea Hags who definitely wanted us dead.

This, of course, wasn't good for business. We had actual *paying* customers on the island for the first time in months. However, if they were watching the deadly showdown from the beach, I was certain they would be departing immediately.

"Take that!" Ariel growled as she twisted out of the deadly embrace of a Sea Hag and beheaded it with her sharp fin.

"Only a few left. We've got this," I shouted as I dove under a wave to avoid a trio of Hag daggers tossed my way.

The salty air was polluted with the acrid odor of Sea Hag BO and stanky breath that would make one weep. It wasn't fair. All we wanted to do was live quietly on our island and have some fun. Being attacked by greedy Sea Hags who were trying to take over the Bermuda Triangle wasn't part of the plan. They'd already taken possession of the two neighboring Mermaid islands and now they were after ours.

Not gonna happen.

I'd welcomed the displaced Mermaids, but it was getting a bit overcrowded on our small parcel of tropical paradise. Whatever. I had no plans to get kicked off of the place we'd called home for the last century. Plugging my nose to avoid the stench, I went for the remaining Sea Hag—of course there were, unfortunately, more where she'd come from but we'd almost dispensed of the twelve that had staged today's invasion.

Swimming at a speed that almost rendered me invisible, I headbutted the disgusting excuse of a creature and she went flying out of the ocean like a shot from a cannon. Her scream was music to my ears. The force of my attack knocked her arms off. This was excellent. An armless Sea Hag couldn't throw spells—or Hag daggers. She elevated out of the water about a hundred feet and narrowed her eyes menacingly.

"Bony Velma Dustface demands your surrender," the toothless Hag hissed as she pointed at me with the toe of her slimy boot. Since her arms were absent, it was all she had. It looked ridiculous.

"You can tell Bony Velma Buttface that she can shove it," I roared, setting the surface of the sea on fire and watching the Sea Hag scream with fury.

"It's Dustface, you rude half-fish," the Sea Hag growled, staying far above the enchanted flames I'd set.

"That's what I said," I replied, flipping the idiot the bird.

"You said Buttface."

"Nope," I argued. "Clearly you have water in your ears. I said Slutcase."

"I was pretty sure you said Nutpaste," Ariel volunteered with a wide irreverent grin.

"Enough. You will be sorry, Tallulah of the Mystical Isle Pod. You will rue the day you were born," she shrieked.

"At least I wasn't hatched, Rickety Shelia Clotlegs," I snarled and silently summoned the sharks.

The sharks despised eating Sea Hags. According to my hammerhead buddies, the Hags tasted like butt. I was completely and happily unaware of what butt tasted like, but I took my friends' word for it. I would owe them big for getting rid of the dead Hags, but odiferous bodies washing up on the beach wasn't real appealing to tourists.

"Be gone, you abomination," I shouted as I waved my hand and created a strong wind sending the flames higher. "Go back to your cave and tell your leader that she can fuck herself."

"Psst," Misty said, swimming up to me. "They actually *can* fuck themselves. Might want to pick another threat."

"Are you serious?" I whispered. "How did I not know this?"

Misty shrugged. "No clue, dudette. You want me to tell her off?"

"Umm, sure," I said, still trying to absorb the appalling fact that Sea Hags could *do* themselves. I supposed it was probably a good thing since no creature in their right mind would want to get within a hundred feet of the hideous beasts.

"Tell old Bony Velma that her farts are so bad she's been accused of Global Warming. I'd suggest you *losers* go into hiding before the Stank Patrol arrests your asses," Misty shouted with a snort of delight, as Rickety Sheila Clotlegs shrieked with fury.

"I will be back and you will be sorry," she bellowed as she disappeared in a blast of putrid green mist, leaving her fallen comrades floating on the water.

"Did you call the sharks or do we have to clean this shitshow up?" Madison asked, swimming over.

"They'll be here in five," I replied.

"TALLULAH," ARIEL GRIPED, WIPING THE BLOOD FROM HER sparkling orange tail as we made our way to shallower waters. "I don't know how much longer we can hold the Hags off. Our morale is shit, I've lost about twenty scales and the humans have all but left the island. Our tourist business is sucking the big one."

Sighing, I looked at my tiny, battered army of exhausted Mermaids. There were four of us including me. At the moment, it was my sisters and me against a giant army of stinky foes. I was the oldest of my siblings and therefore I got stuck with being the leader. We had others Mermaids in our pod, but we were the only ones strong enough to take on the Hags. The deadly attacks were coming daily and at this point, I wasn't real sure we would live to see next week.

Ariel was correct about our odds and, sadly, our business. Of course her name wasn't really Ariel—it was *Joan*. However, she'd viewed *The Little Mermaid* so many times she'd adopted the name, much to my horror.

"Actually," Madison—whose real name was Cindy, but she was obsessed with the movie *Splash*—chimed in. "Our tourist business has always sucked. Not real sure who thought picking an island smack in the middle of the Bermuda Triangle was a good plan."

"Quit your bitchin'," Misty snapped—the only sister that had kept her given name, besides me. "It was reasonably priced, considering we got robbed by that bastard Pirate that Tallulah was boinking a century ago and we had no gold coins left to buy something in a better location."

"Ya know," I said, running my hands through my lavender hair and rolling my matching lavender eyes. "It's not like I'm the only one who boinked an asshole over the centuries—we're Mermaids—we tend to boink fairly often. Ariel, I believe we just had to take out a *restraining order* on the Johnny Depp wannabe who trashed the gift shop and peed in the pool when the cruise ship stopped by—ensuring that we are no longer a destination for any of the cruise ship lines."

Ariel shrugged her slim shoulders and tossed her bright blue hair over her shoulders. "He was hot," she said in her defense and then giggled. "And a total douche."

"And Madison," I pointed out, tired of being blamed for our bad fortune. "You boinked the Dragon Twins who literally fried the entire south end of the island."

"Fine point. Well made," Madison agreed with a shudder. "Although it's too bad that was five years ago. We could certainly use those fire breathers now. It would be fabulous to fry up some Sea Hag and feed it to the sharks."

"True," I said with a weary chuckle. "However, I've made a call for back up."

My Sisters of the Sea stared at me in shock.

"What?" I demanded, slapping my tail on the surface of the water and splashing the open mouthed dummies.

"How exactly are we going to pay for backup?" Misty asked. "We're kinda low in the bank department."

"I have a plan," I started only to be met with groans from the ungrateful idiots I presided over.

"Does this *plan* have anything to do with magicians who

incite terror in humans and create massive lawsuits?" Madison inquired with a snicker.

"No," I snapped. "And Merlin couldn't help the way he looked. Of course, sawing the human newlyweds in half was a horrifying idea, but other than that he was lovely."

"He was a twelve hundred year old jackhole," Ariel pointed out.

"Fine. He was a mistake," I admitted. "I just thought we needed some entertainment for the humans. Hindsight is twenty-twenty. I fired him and I was able to repair the couple he dismembered."

"What's your plan?" Madison asked as she plucked a shrimp from the sea and popped it into her mouth. "Needs cocktail sauce," she muttered, spitting it back out.

Ignoring her appalling manners, I continued trying to drum up some excitement. "The Hags have an enormous stash of diamonds in their cave. As you can plainly see, the damage they've caused to our island makes it only right that we should be compensated for their destruction. And if what I hear is true there will be plenty left over to pay for whomever is being sent to us."

"Hang on a second," Misty said, narrowing her emerald green eyes that were identical in color to her long curly locks. "You called for backup and you have no clue who you called?"

"I called the Otherworld Defense Agency. The human owner—Renee—was lovely and promised to send a crew that was good on the sea and deadly."

Misty's point hit home in an enormous way. It was insanely irresponsible of me to have agreed to just anyone. However, the Renee woman wasn't sure who she could find to help us. Desperate times called for shitty measures. Any help would do at this point.

"Better not be fucking Pirates," Madison grumbled as she waved her hand over her tail and conjured her human legs.

"Pirates hate Mermaids and Mermaids hate Pirates—or at least we do," Misty stated as she too took on her land body. "Hopefully, they'll send Selkies. I'm horny and those bastards are hot."

"As long as it's not Sponge Bob Square Pants, we'll be fine," I said with a laugh as I reluctantly called to my land legs. Being in the water was where I longed to be, but I had a pod to lead and we needed to prepare a few rooms at the crumbling lodge for our mystery hired guns. It hadn't even occurred to me that Renee could send Pirates. My distress call was a last ditch effort to save my people, our home and our pathetic business.

Besides, it wouldn't be the one Pirate that I despised more than any other. He would be an idiot to show his face here after what he'd done. Not only did the dumbass abscond with our treasure, the son of a bitch took my heart with him as well.

I'd tear his sorry ass to shreds if he so much as stepped on my island.

3

PIRATE DOUG

I STARED AT MY THREE-MAN CREW AND SIGHED DRAMATICALLY. They stood in a row, all looking extremely guilty—*because they were.* I'd been sailing the seven seas with the arseholes for two hundred years. I expected better of my mates.

Thornycraft 'Gunner' Rowley stared at his fingers. He was missing three of them and his thumb so at least that made some sense to me. However, Bonar 'Savage' Thunder and Upton 'Iron Chest' Driscol had no such excuse. They were sporting all of their fucking digits.

"Who thought calling my inebriated father was an outstanding idea?" I demanded as I paced the small cabin below the main deck of the ship.

"He did," they all yelled, pointing at each other.

"Did not, ya greasy haired sea rat," Upton bellowed at his comrades.

"Wasn't me," Bonar swore and narrowed his eyes at the others.

"Yarr are peg-legged bow bunglers," Thornycraft shouted, pointing at the idiots—or at least he tried. Being partially fingerless had some distinct disadvantages.

I paused for a long moment and rolled my eyes. "What the hell does *peg-legged bow bunglers* even mean?"

All three stared at each other in confusion as they searched for the answer. Some things were simply better left to the imagination. Deciding it was counterproductive to flummox them even more—not to mention I was also a bit bewildered at this point—I got back to the matter at hand.

"So if none of you arses called my father. Who did?" I demanded.

As if on cue, the bane of my fucking existence—or at least one of them—swooped into the cabin and landed on my shoulder.

"Holly, how many times do I have to tell you that you are not allowed in the house?" I growled, attempting to remain stoic as the scraggly feathered flying shitbag dug her sharp claws into my shoulder and sent an electrical shock through my body.

"Ahoy, Dipshit," the parrot chirped and dug her claws in deeper.

"Ahh, Captain?" Upton said raising his hand politely.

"Yes, Upton?" I asked, trying not to wince as the vicious avian pecked at my ear.

"The bird's name is Polly—not Holly."

"Interesting," I replied, trying to recall if Upton was correct.

For the life of me, I could never remember the moniker of the pest. It had barnacled itself to me fifty years ago. No matter how many times I'd tried to kill it or leave it in a random port, the soaring shitter always found her way back.

"Are you sure?" I asked, wondering if I could pawn the little bastard off on my father.

"Aye, Captain," Upton replied, keeping his distance.

Polly or Holly—I still wasn't convinced—was known to go for the eyes and occasionally, the nuts. A smart man kept a healthy distance from the maniac.

"So Solly," I growled at the bird.

"Polly," Bonar corrected me.

"Right. *Polly,*" I amended. "Are you the scurvy wench that invited my father aboard my ship?"

"Eat me, arsehole," she chirped and crapped on my shoulder.

The crew stayed warily silent as did I. Thankfully, there had been a pause before the *arsehole* part of that comment, but I was unsure if she was calling me an arsehole or wanted me to eat hers. The thought was appalling and it was all I could do not to remove my own arm and beat her with it.

"Umm," I said, carefully gauging my next move. "I've already had breakfast so I'll have to pass. Answer the question or I'll feed you to the sharks."

Not that my shark friends wanted anything to do with Polly-Holly-Solly either. They were as terrified of her as we were. The damned bird made the bloodthirsty Gnomes seem like innocent children.

"You're a dumbarse," Polly cawed and flapped her wings in my face.

"Your point?" I inquired with an eye roll. I already knew this. I wanted to know if the feathered fiend had called my father. The bird was an idiot.

"Polly want a cracker, douchebucket."

"What the hell is a cracker douchebucket?" I asked my wide-eyed, cowardly crew who were slowly making their way to the door of the cabin.

"Well..." Thornycraft said, scratching his head. "Me guess would be it's a vinegar hamper used to hold salted biscuits."

"Do we have one of those?" I asked, certain Thornycraft was correct.

He was excellent with random bits of bizarre knowledge.

"I do," Upton announced.

"Go get it, man," I shouted. "Wally is trying to gouge my shoulder off. I'm dying here."

"'Tis impossible, Captain," Bonar said. "The parrot would have to behead ye to actually end yer life."

"It was a finger of speech," I snapped. "Certainly you've heard of that."

"A finger?" Thornycraft asked, squinting his eyes and pointing to the invisible digits on his hand. "I thought it was a *figure* of speech."

"Don't think. It's overrated. Get the damned vinegar cookie basket. NOW."

My crew sprinted from the cabin like the Devil himself was on their heels. Damn it. I was alone with the bird. I thought the surprise visit from my father was hideous, but no, this was much worse.

"So Folly, nice weather we're having," I said, keeping the conversation neutral.

"Yep, Doug," the feathered jackhole replied.

"It's *Pirate Doug*. If you're going to terrorize my ship you will call me by the correct name, Yolly," I told her. No one called me *Doug* and lived to tell.

Lolly's eye roll was outstanding. "Pot. Kettle. Black," she squawked and flipped me off.

"Whatever," I muttered, conceding the point. She'd called me *Doug* to be disrespectful. I called her Dolly because I couldn't for the life of me remember her name. There was a distinct difference here. Anyhoo, I had a much bigger problem at the moment and I was fairly sure Nolly was at the root of it.

"Umm… I understand my father is on deck. Do you know why he's here?"

"Yep."

"Would you like to share?" I asked carefully as I coaxed the bird to my hand.

"Nope," the parrot answered, settling herself on my arm and piercing an artery.

"Do you hate me?" I asked through gritted teeth, wondering if I snapped her neck if she would survive it.

"Yar Dipshit, gotta feed the fish. Yarr are a mutiny minded platoon splinter. Yar will dance the hempen jig and walk the plank if yar cutlass flappin' fish stink don't avast ye," she squawked.

"My arse is in danger?" I asked, trying to decipher her babbling. The vicious bird was more fluent in Pirate speak than I was.

With a swift swat to the back of my head with her wing, I went flying across the cabin. I was a damned Vampire Pirate and I was getting my arse handed to me by a bird. It was a fine thing that my crew wasn't present.

"Talk to yer dad," Bolly squawked, pointing her wing at me.

"Now?" I questioned, hoping to delay what was most definitely going to be a mortifying heart to heart with my father.

I had Sea Hags to destroy and a certain Mermaid to dodge. I didn't have time for family reunions at the moment.

"NOW!" the feathered menace instructed.

She didn't have to ask twice. Quickly waving a hand over my gushing artery, I stemmed the flow of blood and checked myself in the mirror. Damn, if I wasn't a handsome son of a bitch. I could take on the world today.

Or at least I could take on my father... maybe...

4

PIRATE DOUG

"I'D REALLY LIKE YOU TO CALL ME PAPPY," POSEIDON BELLOWED, uncorking a bottle of my finest rum and dancing around the deck of my ship like he needed to be medicated.

His Clam Band—whom he always traveled with and were literally six clams with arms and legs—played a teeth grinding medley of banjo tunes and grinned with delight at the bizarre antics of my insane father. Fish were jumping out of the water to catch a glimpse of the God of the Sea and the old man didn't disappoint. He danced like a loon until he'd worked up a sweat and then doused his body with my fucking rum.

The man was enormous and terrifying. I'd often considered suggesting he dye his arse length green hair a more appealing color, but his wrath was legendary. I'd long ago decided to keep my fashion tips to myself. While my intellect might be questionable, my memory was excellent. I was still sporting a nasty scar from the time I'd offered up my opinion on his wearing a toga and what amounted to a diaper in the winter. *Pappy's* attempts at getting closer over the centuries were becoming more frequent—and more alarming.

"Okay... *Pappy,*" I said slowly, savoring the word on my tongue. I liked it. "How about Pappy Poseidon?"

"How about no?" he shot back and took a healthy swig from the bottle. "I've come to apologize for ruining your life and to warn you about your future."

"How about we just get wasted and call it a day?" I suggested gamely. Conversation never ended well for us. I usually ended up blowing one of my ships to smithereens in a temper tantrum when my father was about.

"While that appeals greatly, I have come for a reason. My therapist thinks that honesty is important. I have my doubts, but she is quite attractive with lovely bosoms so I'm going to give it a shot. *Sit,* boy."

I did. I might be a five hundred year old Vampire Pirate, but when Poseidon told you to sit—you sat.

"Alrighty then," he said, shrugging out of his rum soaked toga and tossing it overboard to the squealing female fish who followed him everywhere. "Son, I never intended for you to end up an undead bloodsucker of the Seven Seas."

My eyes narrowed to slits. We'd been through this one before. I quite enjoyed being a Vampire. I had no idea how I'd become a Vamp, but the perks were fabulous. Yessss, I had to wear sunscreen—SPF 100 for total blockage—due to the burning to a crisp in the sunlight issue, but my regenerative powers were outstanding.

"Great. Apology accepted," I said through clenched teeth. "Next?"

It wasn't exactly wise to have a go at the God of the Sea, but I was going to do exactly that if the old man kept it up. If he really wanted to be *honest* he'd tell me who my damned mother was.

"Let me explain," he continued with a chuckle. "I lost the Championship Olympian Charades Tournament about four hundred and seventy-two years ago which was utter bullshit considering I'm brilliant with pantomime. Who do you think taught Marcel Marceau all his moves? I'm still certain that bastard Zeus cheated, but that drunken sot Dionysus was judging and I think Zeus bribed him."

"Does this have a point?" I asked with an eye roll.

"Of course it does," Poseidon bellowed and finished off the rum. "Since I lost, I had to hand over my favorite child to be turned into a Vampire."

"Seriously?" I questioned. The Gods were indeed crazy. Not that I was unhappy with the end result, but that was one fucked up game of charades.

"Yes," he said sheepishly as my bird Rolly dive bombed him and crapped on his head.

It was the first nice thing the airborne shit monster had ever done for me. I grinned and gave the bird a thumbs up. However, since she was such an evil piece of work, she took a flying dump on me as well.

"Of course, I didn't really think it all through. And as your mother—the greatest love of my life—was out shopping, I just grabbed you from the top of the pile and let them turn you," he finished and then popped open another bottle of rum.

"Interesting," I said, taking the bottle from his hand and downing half the contents. It was very difficult to tie one on for a Vampire, but a bit of liquid courage at the moment was necessary. "And my mother's name?"

"All in good time, son," Poseidon assured me as he signaled to his Clam Band. They began strumming a horrifying banjo medley of Phil Collins' greatest hits. "Just know that your mother has been watching your every move for quite some time now."

"That sounds rather frightening," I choked out, glancing around for someone who could pass as my mother. I certainly hoped it wasn't one of the clams.

"Trust me, boy," Poseidon affirmed. "It scares the hell out of me too. The crazy harpy tries to castrate me every chance she gets. But the woman loves you something fierce. She cut a bizarre deal with Apollo to get permission to guard over you."

"Why does the woman not show her face?" I demanded.

Pappy Poseidon shrugged his wide shoulders and sighed. "That I don't know. However, you will know her when you meet her."

"How?"

"She's rather violent and has the mouth of a sailor," he replied with a shudder. "Now on to the rest of the reason I'm here—besides the fact that you have outstanding rum. You need to beware the Kraken. The multi-legged menace is after my successor."

"So why are you warning *me*?" I demanded. I really didn't have time for this shit. I needed to get the mission done while keeping my pecker intact. This would get the Gnomes off my arse and then I could make a looting schedule for the summer. I was very busy.

"Are ya daft, boy?" Pappy shouted, slapping himself on the forehead and groaning. "*You*. You're my successor—not that I'm going to retire anytime soon in the next millennia, but all Gods have heirs."

"An heir and a spare?" I questioned, hoping one of the other nine hundred and twenty of my siblings might be ahead of me.

"You are my favorite, Pirate Doug," Poseidon replied. "You will take my place. However, you need to get your shit together and become the god-in-training I know you can be."

"Could you be a bit more specific?" I inquired. If having arse length green hair was part of the job description I was going to pass.

Poseidon looked to the sky and shook his enormous head. "You need to settle down with a nice immortal gal and quit your pilfering."

My eyes narrowed and my fingers began to spit menacing sparks. "I'm quite good at pilfering and I enjoy it."

"Yes well, you also have as many bounties on your head as you have brothers and sisters," Pappy pointed out with a raised brow.

"Your point?"

"My point is that you will keep your eyes open for the Kraken. That giant ugly squid bastard is a deadly foe. I haven't groomed you for nearly five hundred years to have you end up being lunch for that Titan son of a bitch. You feel me?"

"I do," I replied, warming to the idea of eventually taking over for the old man. Looting the other Gods was wildly appealing. "I shall be on watch for the Smacken."

"Kraken," Pappy said.

"Right. Kraken. Anything else?" I inquired.

"Yes. The one you are meant for hates your scoundrel guts. You shall need to prove your worth to her and her kind. This is important, boy. The Gods have decided the time has come for you to settle your randy ass down. Of course, the simpletons also thought it was a fine plan to turn you into a Vampire, but that's neither here nor there at the moment."

"That's a little vague." I wasn't quite sure if I could get away with avoiding the command. I was outstanding at shirking responsibility... and looting... and fornicating.

"Yep, I'm good like that. Besides that's all I know. Who exactly have you been seeing as of late?" Pappy asked.

"Define *seeing*," I said.

"Manwhore," my unwanted sidekick squawked and crossed her scraggly wings over her puffed up chest in disgust.

"Interesting," Pappy said with a wide grin. "Well, I'd suggest you make a list of the women who despise you and then work your way down until you find your mate."

"That could take a while," I explained.

"A long, long, long, long, long, long..." the obnoxious bird chirped with a parrot cackle.

"Enough, Jolly," I shouted. "The ladies love me! I'm Pirate Doug. My trouser snake is legendary and my staying power is unrivaled. I shall be able to figure this new conundrum out. I'm not stellar at math, but Upton has a calculator and says he knows how to use it."

"Dipshit," the parrot sang as she lit up like a deranged firework and bit a chunk of hair from my head. "Prove it."

My Pappy was smart enough to run for cover and his Clam Band dove back into the ocean, banjos and all. Of course, my idiot crew was still nowhere to be seen. I just hoped the arses had found the cracker douchebucket. Dolly was on a rampage.

"I shall prove it," I swore as I dove under a pile of ropes and hid from the bird. "You just wait, you hateful bag of feathers. I shall find my mate."

5

TALLULAH

"They left," Misty said, letting her head drop forward in defeat. "I tried to get them to stay on—even offered them a free week at the lodge—but no go."

I sighed as I tried to balance our books. Motherhumpin' chicken of the sea, we were barely making it before the Sea Hags had terrorized our island. Now we were about to lose our shirts—not that we wore shirts. Bikini tops were more to our liking. Our hair and our eyes were set from birth. My color was lavender, Ariel's was blue, Misty's was emerald green and Madison's was pink. Each Mermaid's hair and eyes were unique to them and no two were alike. However, the color of our tails changed with our moods and our fashion choices. I always matched my tail—or when in human form, my sarong skirt— to my bikini top.

"*All* the humans are gone?" I asked.

"Every last one."

"That's probably better," I said with a wide smile that I hoped didn't look like a pained grimace. I was trying my damnedest to be positive. "As soon as our mystery backup arrives, we can destroy the Hags and then business will pick up. We'll be saving money if we don't have to ship in human food for a little while and I'll temporarily suspend everyone's salary—not that anyone has actually gotten paid in a year or two."

"Or three," Misty said with a grin.

"Of four," I corrected her with a giggle.

"Don't worry," Misty said, putting her arms around me and hugging me tight. "We'll be fine. If not, we can go back to Vegas and work in the Cirque Du Soleil water show again. That was fun and I got laid regularly."

"You're right. We're Mermaids. Our kind has survived for thousands of years. We will not let a little setback get us down like no money, or a war with the Sea Hags, or a shittily located island or dire lack of beddable men. Of course, dying would suck."

"Speak for yourself," Misty said with a raised brow.

"You don't think dying would suck?" I questioned, confused.

"Oh, that would definitely suck. However, you're the only one lacking in the beddable men department. When was the last time you did the nasty?" Misty inquired.

"It was… umm… it must have been…"

"Dudette," Misty said with a laugh. "Suffice it to say it's been far too long since someone caught your eye and warmed your bed."

I was silent because she was correct. Mermaids were the sirens of the sea. It was our calling to lure men in and indulge in hedonistic pleasure. In the olden days before my time—*thank Poseidon*—our kind used to ingest their paramours after seducing them. Now we were just normal gals with tails, very long lives—and healthy libidos.

And I had definitely been ignoring mine.

I just hadn't found myself attracted to anyone in eons. However, it was time to change that sad fact. Maybe our saviors would be attractive. I could see myself with a hot Selkie or even a Werewolf as long as he wasn't too hairy. Our luck was changing. I could feel it in my fins.

Today was the day I started living again.

"THEY'RE COMING," ARIEL SHOUTED AS THE MERMAIDS SQUEALED and assembled on the beach.

Our pod was small—only fifteen—but with all the homeless Mermaids in the Bermuda Triangle shacking up with us at the moment our number had reached about a hundred. It was getting increasingly difficult to house all of the displaced gals, but thankfully many enjoyed slumbering in the pool. At least fifty slept in the Olympic sized pool at night and about fifteen caught their Z's in the hot tub. It wasn't the best situation, but we were making do.

"Ohhhh," a Mermaid with bright orange hair from a neighboring island cooed, shuddering with delight and adjusting her bikini top so her breasts were literally popping out of it. "Men on a ship!"

As if on cue, about eighty of the horny idiots dropped their tops and began jumping up and down. I was surprised a few didn't knock themselves out with the size of their assets.

Rolling my eyes and looking up to the Heavens, I reminded myself that it would be bad form to annihilate my species just because the vast majority were loose in the morals department. I had my hands full at the moment. There was no way in Poseidon's Seven Seas I could teach my kind to behave in a ladylike manner in five minutes.

"Nope," I shouted and shot a warning blast of purple magic

into the air. "These men are not here for our pleasure or theirs. They are here to help us fight off the Sea Hags. If anyone so much as flashes a tit at them, I will put you in the Under Water Pokey. Am I clear?"

Nodding unhappily, the masses covered up their goodies and pouted. It was difficult leading hordes of horny women, but I wasn't bullshitting them. I'd incarcerate any randy swimming hooker who derailed my plans to save the island. Sadly, most of the Mermaids on the beach were worthless in the fighting department. It was why the Hags had been successful at taking over their islands. We were created by Poseidon for pleasure—not war. However, some of us had evolved with necessity and the Mermaids of the Mystical Isle Pod had definitely rolled with the tide.

"What the ever-lovin' tuna?" Ariel muttered, squinting out at the slowly approaching ship. "Is that a Pirate ship?"

"Looks like it," Madison said with a shit-eating grin. "And that flag looks vaguely familiar. Don't ya think so, Tallulah?"

I froze and glared at the ship out on the horizon. This could not be happening. Of all the freakin' deadly immortals that could have been sent to help, it had to be *him*? Did the nimrod have a death wish? Was he unaware of whom he'd agreed to aid? Was he simply an idiot?

I quickly pushed away the ridiculous zing of pleasure that sizzled through me at the thought of seeing the sticky-fingered imbecile again and instead focused on dismembering the son of a bitch. Fool me once, shame on me. Fool me twice, lose your joystick.

"Mother of Pearl in a jock strap," I hissed, doing a few jumping jacks to get limbered up. "Sorry, but I'm gonna have to kill the backup. Maybe if we teach the hookers on the beach to fight, we can take the Sea Hags without help."

"Whoa, whoa, whoa," Misty said with wide eyes and a grunt of laughter. "How about we let Pirate Slug and his crew of dummies help us defeat the Hags and *then* we off them? Not sure there's enough time in the near future to train an army of gals who would rather be painting their nails than fighting."

"Point," I agreed as the blood pumped through my veins and my adrenaline spiked. "Can I deck him though?"

"Absolutely," Ariel said. "We'll help."

"No," I said as my lavender locks began to blow around my head and my magic drew close to the surface. "He's all mine."

Pirate Doug was about to rue the day he'd been born.

"Wait, what the hell is happening out there?" I asked as the sea whipped up into a violent storm and tossed the ship full of idiots around like rag dolls.

"Did you cause a hurricane?" Misty asked, watching in shock as enormous waves almost capsized the ship.

"Nope, not that I wouldn't like to, but we're kind of screwed at the moment. I was going with the plan to kill them *after* they help us," I said, wondering what to do.

"Do you think it's the Sea Hags?" Madison asked.

"Doubtful. Those stinky buttcracks don't have that much power," I replied.

"What kind of creature can cause that kind of damage?" Ariel inquired.

"Well, umm… Pirates can," I said with an eye roll and a shake of my head.

"Are they that stupid? I mean, they're about a mile offshore. Did they think that forcing us to save their asses would be impressive?" Misty asked as she winced at the violent show we were observing.

"We're not going anywhere," I lied through my teeth. "If those idiots can't sail a ship, they sure as hell can't fight off Sea Hags."

My sisters just stared at me and I let my chin fall to my chest.

"Fine," I conceded. "If the ship goes down we can drag them in. But no one touches Pirate Doug but me. Clear?"

"Roger that," Misty said with a wink. "Pirate Doug is all yours."

6

PIRATE DOUG

"FUCKING KRAKEN," I BELLOWED AS I WAVED MY HANDS IN THE air and summoned a hurricane. The multi-legged bastard had been chasing us for three hundred nautical miles and the ship was bearing the brunt of the maniac's wrath. I knew we would have a chilly reception from the Mermaids, but bringing a man-eating Kraken to their shores would not bode well for anyone's peckers at all.

"Solly, make yourself useful. Crap on the arsehole's head," I commanded.

The damned bird perked up and laid a few outstanding turds on Bonar's bald head.

"Not *that* arsehole," I shouted above the wind of the storm I'd created to blow the Kraken back out to sea. "The arsehole in the water that's trying to sink the damned frigate."

With a disrespectful wiggle of her tail feathers, Dolly called me a few unmentionable names and shot straight up into the air like a bullet from a pistol. The scraggly shitter paused only momentarily about two hundred feet in the air and then flew straight at the Kraken. As she barreled down toward the beast her beak grew in size. It was fabulously nightmare inducing.

The damned beak looked like an oddly shaped, orange, twenty-foot long dagger.

"Yarr a green gilled, cutlass flapping, soaked shitbucket," Jolly screeched as she jammed her massive beak right between the beast's eyes.

The Kraken screamed like a girl and tried to knock my bird off his warty, slimy, puke green body, but Wally wasn't having it. She added her claws to the mix and sent an electrical shock through the monster that turned his blubbery green skin a solid, ashy white. It looked like an enormous albino octopus.

Tolly pulled her beak out and with a quick and impressive crap on the Kraken's head, flew back to the ship. With one last roar, the Kraken sank under the waves and swam back out to sea.

My men and I were shocked to a horrified yet wildly impressed silence as Golly landed on the poop deck and flipped us off. Thankfully her beak was back to normal size. I was beginning to doubt that my bird was a bird at all, but I had no time to ponder that conundrum. Thinking was draining and I needed my energy to conjure up some pecker protectors. I'd mull over Zolly's quirks later—or never. It was quite possible that I didn't want to solve the secret of Colly. Something in my gut told me it would not bode well.

"Upton, get yer arse to the crow's nest and tell me what you see," I instructed as I snapped my fingers and abruptly ended the hurricane.

"Crayons with boobs, Captain," he shouted down at us with a grin on his face.

"Sexist pig humper," Molly squawked and flew out ahead of the ship towards the island.

Her parting gift was a turd atop each of our heads. We were definitely going to have to take a dip before we hit shore or we'd smell like bird droppings.

"Explain yourself, man," I demanded, squinting my eyes at

the island in the distance and trying to make out what the idiot saw. Had we gone off course and aimed for the wrong island? I was an excellent navigator, but the Kraken had demanded all my attention. We could have easily taken a wrong turn somewhere along the way.

"About a hundred Mermaids. All different colors. Looks like an ocean of crayons with tremendous knockers."

"Aye." I nodded in understanding. "Do you see one with lavender hair and a rack that could make a grown man weep?"

"Front and center," Upton replied with a shudder. "Looks kinda mean—and kinda familiar."

Thornycraft raised his hand politely and waited to be called on.

"Yes?"

"Is thar a reason yarr going to an island where I'm fairly sure the mutiny minded She-Devils inhabiting it want to put us in Davy Jones' locker?"

"Fine question, mate," I replied, realizing I'd completely forgotten to get my crew up to speed on the dangerous mission we were about to embark on. Between my Pappy's visit, thoughts of a certain sexy Mermaid I'd wronged taking revenge on my nads, and Rolly being on a turd dropping rampage, I'd been a bit scattered. "I cut a fine deal to get the Gnomes off my arse. However, it involves saving the testicle-bashing Mermaids from the Sea Hags."

"Can we loot 'em?" Bonar inquired, very logically.

"Only the Hags," I explained. "But I'm warning ya now, keep your nuts out of range of the colorful swimming hookers. It takes months to regrow a tallywhacker."

My men nodded solemnly and placed their hands over their jewels.

"Just follow my lead and we'll be out of here in a jiffy," I promised.

"Correct me if I'm wrong," Upton said with a smirk. "But

me thinks there might be a swimming hooker on that thar isle that hates yer guts."

"Your point?" I asked with an eye roll. There was no way in Poseidon's Seas I was going to let on that I was looking forward to seeing the half-woman, half-fish that I'd never been able to forget.

"Overheard yer Pappy tell you that yer true mate hates yer guts," Upton offered up with a raised brow.

An unfamiliar burst of elation burst consumed me, but then fear for my manhood outweighed it by a ten ton whale. "Fate couldn't be such an arse to barnacle me to a woman who would just as soon tear my schlong off and throw it to the sharks as warm my bed," I blustered.

My brain told me this was a bad thing, but my roger grew *quite* jolly at the thought of Tallulah.

"But wait," Thornycraft said, scratching his head with the hand that had fingers on it. "Didn't ye pilfer all the gold coins from this particular man-eating pod?"

"I might have," I muttered, examining my nails nonchalantly. "Can't quite recall."

"Yar did," Bonar said with a laugh. "Yar got some booty and then took off with some booty."

The idiots thought that was hilarious. At the time, it had seemed quite logical. Now? Not so much.

"Enough," I growled. "Tallulah probably doesn't even remember that I absconded with their treasure. Certainly a hundred years is enough time to forgive a little boo-boo."

"If yar says so," Thornycraft said with a barely suppressed chuckle as he tossed me his spyglass. "But the She-Devil don't look like she forgot."

Peeking through the lens, my breath caught in my throat.

Tallulah of the Mystical Isle Pod was the most tremendous specimen of a female that the Gods had ever created. Her full, pouty lips were made to be kissed and her body was made for lovin'. My fingers itched to bury themselves in her long lavender locks almost as much as my trouser snake longed to be buried in her luscious body.

The Mermaid's sun kissed skin glistened and her eyes...

Well, they were narrowed to slits of rage. My crew was correct. Clearly, the swimming sexpot had a sharp memory. What in the sea-loving hell had I been thinking to leave such a delicious, pissed off wench behind? Maybe it wasn't such a bad thing she hated my guts.

Maybe.

7

TALLULAH

"AND THAT'S FOR STEALING OUR GOLD COINS YOU WORM-RIDDLED fish gizzard," I hissed as I landed an excellent left hook to the face of the bastard who'd betrayed me.

The sound of the punch as it connected was excellent and Pirate Doug went flying across the sand. The look of surprised shock on his stupidly handsome face was gratifying but I wasn't even close to done yet.

Sadly, the son of a bitch was as gorgeous as I'd remembered —six foot four of dark-haired, dark-eyed, muscly man. Since he and his questionably intelligent crew had moored the ship a couple hundred feet offshore and swam in, his clothes were plastered to his perfect body—every damned lickable muscle was evident. His lips were so pretty they belonged on a woman and his lashes were so long they made me jealous. My lady bits were definitely awake and my innate seductive nature was simmering hot under the surface. However, I wasn't about to fall into the arms or the bed of the lying, cheating idiot.

"At least she didn't go for my nuts! I call that a win," Pirate Doug yelled happily to his crew of three as he picked himself up off the ground and bowed gallantly to me. "Ahhh, Tallulah of the Mystical Isle Pod of swimming hookers, you're as hot-tempered and pokable as I recall."

"And you're as disgusting as you were a hundred years ago," I snapped, crossing my arms over my chest to hide my traitorous perky nipples. Why in the heck couldn't I be attracted to some nice, boring, dependable Merman? Why did I get all hot and bothered for an asswipe of epic proportions? The cretin had just called me a hooker and made it sound freakin' flattering.

"Thank you," he replied with a panty melting grin that definitely didn't go unnoticed by the horny Mermaids on the beach.

"Wasn't a compliment, jackass," I replied, biting back a smile.

Someone had smacked the idiot with a charm stick the day he was born and he was outstanding at using his talent. Of course he was talented in other areas as well, but I refused to go there.

"So I take it you *hate* me," he stated, looking bizarrely hopeful while approaching me warily.

"Ya think, you hat of ass?" I snapped. To make sure he understood, I kicked his legs out from underneath him as his men stood by and did nothing except grin at their captain having his butt handed to him.

Pirates were insane and Vampires were certifiable. I had no clue what the origin of his crew was, but Doug was a Pirate Vamp—an obnoxious, sticky fingered, well-endowed, undead jackass. I knew for certain that he could take me out with a wave of his powerfully magical hand. However, I also knew somewhere inside my furious head that he would never harm me—physically that is. He might rob me blind, but he would never harm me.

"Excellent news," Pirate Doug bellowed as he got to his feet and dusted the sand off the ridiculous steel pecker protector he was wearing.

"And how exactly is that excellent news?" I asked, wondering if I would break my foot if I kicked him in the nuts. The metal manhood cover appeared fairly solid.

"The search is over, boys," he informed his men as they gave him thumbs up. "I have found her. Upton, we shall not be needing your calculator."

"Aye, Captain," Upton said with a wide grin. "I wish ye congratulations and will pray to Poseidon for the longevity of yer trouser snake."

"I fear for yer nuggets but feel ye have made a fine choice. The She-Devil does indeed hate yer slimy arse. Congratulations, Captain," Bonar said.

"Yer a brave man to risk yer disco stick, but I understand. If the choice were mine to make, I'd make the same. Or at least me pocket rocket would," Thornycraft stated, saluting his Captain.

"What are you buttheads talking about?" I snapped. "Of course, he found me. I live here, you ignoramuses. You're supposed to help us get the Sea Hags off our backs."

"Piece of cake," Pirate Doug said, looking around at the women who were practically salivating over him.

It was all I could do not to gouge his eyes out. He wasn't supposed to be looking at other Mermaids. He was supposed to be looking at *me*.

Wait... No. I didn't want him. I wanted to castrate him. Why should I care who the stupid gorgeous Pirate looked at?

Still, if he hit on anyone other than me, I would twist that pecker protector into a permanent pretzel.

Wait. I didn't want him to hit on me. I wanted the dumbass to help rid us of the Sea Hags and then I wanted him gone. Forever. I had a freakin' tourist trap to run.

"Seems to me you've added to your pod of swimming

hookers," Pirate Doug observed, turning his attention back to me much to the disappointment of the hookers. "What do you have here? A hundred warriors?"

"Four," I corrected him. "I have four including me. That's part of the problem. There are at least three hundred Hags I know of and possibly more. We've been holding them off as best we can, but it's getting very dicey."

"Have the Hags been multiplying?" Pirate Doug inquired, going a bit pale and gagging.

Clearly he knew how they procreated even if I just learned the unappetizing fact today.

"Sweet Poseidon on a bender," I choked out, going paler than my nemesis. "I certainly hope not."

"Pappy Poseidon is always on a bender," Pirate Doug muttered. "And let's hope the Hags aren't reproducing. It's highly disturbing and very revolting."

Closing my eyes and trying to push the image of Rickety Shelia Clotlegs doing herself out of my frontal lobe, I decided to steer the conversation back to the matter at hand.

"Look, we just need you to help us fight them off," I said, in my most businesslike tone while trying not to stare at his metal Johnson jacket. The apparatus was ridiculous, mostly because his was about three times bigger than the rest of his crew's. "However, you will have to sleep on your ship. You are not to be trusted."

"That's a fine way to treat your fated *mate*," Pirate Doug informed me with a raised brow and a smirk.

My eyes narrowed to slits of rage and the imbecile immediately placed his hands in a protective manner over his steel salami shield. All of the Mermaids on the beach, save Madison, Ariel, and Misty, began to pout and throw mini fits. I was very close to joining them. Pirate Slug had some nerve.

"Are you serious?" I ground out through clenched teeth.

"No, I'm Pirate Doug," he replied with an eye roll.

"No, I meant... never mind," I snapped and shook my head in disbelief. "I am not your mate. I will never be your mate. I hate your guts."

"Fantastic," he bellowed joyously and winked at his crew.

"What part of my last sentence don't you understand?" I demanded.

"Was all of it in English?"

"Yes," I said wondering how many times he'd been dropped on his head as a child.

"Then I comprehended all of it," Pirate Doug announced with satisfaction. Then his eyes grew wide with terror as he pointed frantically to the sky. "Incoming," he screamed and tackled me to the ground.

"What the what?" I grunted as I shoved him off of me and kneed him in the gut.

"Zolly," he wheezed as he again tried to put me underneath him. "She's a vicious flying shitter. I'm saving your life."

"No," I growled as I rolled away before he could trap me beneath him again. I would not admit that I actually enjoyed it. "You're trying to kill me."

"Never," he insisted as he swatted at an adorable parrot that clearly didn't like him any more than I did.

"Stop that," I yelled as I gently took the bird in my arms and cuddled her close. "You do not treat animals like that."

Pirate Doug jumped to his feet and stood frozen in his spot. He watched in awed shock as the poor parrot settled herself on my shoulder and nuzzled my cheek with her soft downy head.

"It's not an animal. It's a maniac turdinator with a foul mouth and claws that will shock your balls off," he whispered with real fear in his voice.

His crew's reaction was similar, except they ran back out to the sea and were swimming back to the ship while shrieking like girls.

"What is *wrong* with you?" I asked. "This is a sweet little thing."

"Pretty Mermaid," the parrot cooed as she stared daggers at the gobsmacked Pirate.

"Ohhhh, she's so cute," Ariel said as she gently scratched under the parrot's chin. "She's too skinny. Let me take her and feed her."

"We have a bucket of crackers in the gift shop," Misty said as she too pet the cooing bird.

"A cracker douchebasket?" Doug inquired hopefully, still whispering.

"What did you just say?" I asked, squinting at him.

"Folly has been inquiring about a vinegar cookie bucket. I have no fucking idea what that is, but if you happen to have one lying around she might stop attacking me. She's a truly terrifying shit monster—craps on me constantly."

"I thought you said her name was Zolly," I said, confused.

"Did I say Zolly?" he asked and then shook his head and chuckled. "I meant Wally."

"You named your female bird *Wally*?" I asked.

"Yes. Is that bad?" he questioned warily. "If it makes it any better, I call her Bolly on Tuesdays and Solly on Saturdays. The flying menace answers to anything."

"He's all yours," Madison said with a laugh and a groan. "Good thing he's not a rocket scientist. We'll take the birdie and you two can talk strategy… or honeymoon plans."

"I'm not his mate," I hissed. "I would rather dismember him than see his member."

"That's not very nice," Pirate Doug pointed out. He backed away as Wally reared up and prepared to attack him.

"Get this straight, you waterlogged weirdo, I am not your mate," I shouted. "I would never spend the rest of my eternal life with a jackhole that robbed me blind and then took off in the middle of the night right after he promised me a romantic Hawaiian vacation. You feel me?"

"So, that's a maybe, right?" Doug said with an adorable look of confusion that made me want to deck him right after I shoved my tongue down his throat.

"Are you daft?" I snapped with an enormous eye roll.

"Define daft," he replied.

"He's not my mate," I insisted to my sisters. "All of the oceans in the world would have to dry up before I agreed to such nonsense."

"Riiight," Ariel said with a wink as she motioned to all the pouty Mermaids on the beach to skedaddle. "We'll be at the lodge."

And they left. I was alone with the man who'd stolen every last cent we'd had and had given me more multiple orgasms than any other. He was all kinds of a jerk and then some— untrustworthy man hooker and annoying.

So why in the Seven Seas did I still want to jump his bones?

8

PIRATE DOUG

"Soooo," I said, trying to gauge if it was safe to remove my hands from my trouser snake. Tallulah was a wild one. "What say you we let bygones be bygones?"

"What say you we get rid of the Hags then you and your crew of weenies leave forever?" she shot back.

"That's one option," I replied with a shrug as I removed my soaked shirt and tossed it to the sand. I knew exactly what I was doing. Her lust-filled scent belied her words and expression. Her quick intake of breath was music to my ears and I considered removing my cojones cover. However, my Mermaid's bite was as violent as her bark. Losing my willy right now would be bad for what I was hoping would transpire.

"You are really something else," she muttered as she ran her hands through her shiny lavender curls and groaned.

"Thank you. I know," I replied.

"That was an insult, Doug."

"My bad," I shot back and then froze. Something strange and surreal was happening in my gut.

For a moment, I wondered if it was the beans I'd eaten for

lunch coming back for a surprise and untimely visit—but no. This was not indigestion. It was something I'd never experienced.

The Mermaid had called me *Doug*... not Pirate Doug... and I liked it. No one in the world could call me Doug and keep my attention, but Tallulah could. Interesting.

"Say that again," I instructed, eyeing her strangely. Was I actually correct about Tallulah being my mate? In all honesty, I just wanted to get my Pappy off my arse. Tallulah was an animal in the sack and delightfully rude. She also fit the criteria of hating me.

Spending eternity with this Mermaid didn't appall me in the least. Could my search be over? Was it this easy? Not that having to guard my pickle for the rest of time would be *easy*. Normally I was consumed with looting riches, not with how to woo a gal, but now I was confused. Nothing new on that front, but...

"Say what again? That you're a dumbass?" she inquired with a laugh.

"No. I am fully aware of that," I told her with a grin. "Say my name."

She considered my request for so long it was downright rude, which of course made my roger even jollier. She was horribly perfect for me. Only downside was that she couldn't see this as well.

"Doug," she finally said.

My pecker protector was now practically choking my Johnson to death. My desire for Tallulah grew along with my willy. What was happening here?

I was speechless and stared at the work of art standing before me. All sorts of unfamiliar feelings consumed me and I was suddenly desperate to know all sorts of things about her.

What was her middle name?

Did she like wasabi with her sushi?

Did she leave the toilet seat up? No. Wait. That was my issue not hers.

Was she team Edward or team Jacob? My mind was a jumbled mess and for the first time in five hundred years I wasn't quite sure how to proceed. I didn't like this at all.

"Crab got your tongue?" Tallulah asked with a smirk that slayed me.

"No," I choked out and weighed how pissed she would be if I suggested we take the conversation to her quarters. "I just... umm..."

"How about this," she suggested, avoiding eye contact. "Let's decide how we're going to deal with the Sea Hags and then you can beg me on bended knee for about a decade or seven to be your mate."

"Will that work?" I asked, feeling hopeful.

"Nope," she replied with a giggle. "But it will be fun."

The Mermaid was lying through her teeth. She was mine. She knew it and I knew it. Or at least I think she knew it. I definitely knew it. Sure I would have to suffer first, but retribution at the hands of my voluptuous Mermaid would certainly include make-up sex. I'd never hung around for make-up sex with anyone, although Cosmopolitan Magazine stated in its prose that it was very hot.

"Fine," I said, adjusting my codpiece so that my bologna pony wouldn't explode and be useless. "Let's make a plan and then I will start begging."

"Vampire Pirates don't beg," Tallulah said, observing me like I was a science experiment gone wrong.

"There's a first time for everything," I replied, snapping my fingers and producing a map of the surrounding islands.

"You're insane."

"Your point?" I asked, spreading the map out on the sand.

"No point. Just an observation," she replied kneeling on the ground next to me.

51

It was going to be extremely difficult to form coherent sentences with all the blood from my brain residing in my tent pole, but I enjoyed a good challenge. Tallulah was about to be mine.

I wasn't quite sure how I was going to accomplish the feat considering I was fairly certain I couldn't take her as my mate unless she agreed. I could always steal her heart if she didn't give it willingly. Looting was my specialty. Love? Not so much. However, I was Pirate Doug, the greatest Vampire Pirate of the Seven Seas. Actually, I was the only Vampire Pirate of the Seven Seas which, in turn, made me the greatest. Or that was the line I was going with.

Now I simply needed to make my Mermaid believe it too. A romp in the sack would be outstanding, but I was certain it was going to take more than that.

What would it take?

No fucking clue. However, being clueless had never stopped me and I had no plans of changing my ways today.

"UPTON," I SAID, PACING THE DECK OF THE SHIP. "HOW WOULD you go about wooing a woman?"

After making preliminary plans to take down the Sea Hags with Tallulah, I'd hightailed it back to the ship to figure out how to win her. Swimming with a thirty-pound pecker protector proved difficult, but I forced myself to swim with ease as my Mermaid was watching. Wouldn't do to drown in her presence.

Upton grinned and settled himself on a lawn chair that we'd pilfered from Target the last time we'd visited Miami. Thornycraft and Bonar were swabbing the deck and eavesdropping, but that was fine. I was going to need as much brainpower as possible with this conundrum.

"Well, Captain," Upton said. "Ye have come to the right seadog for advice on the lasses."

I ignored the muffled laughter of the other idiots and pulled up a matching looted chair.

"Speak, man," I insisted. I was working under a deadline here.

"Are ye talking about getting the wench into yer bed?" Upton questioned.

I paused and considered. That was definitely *part* of the plan. "Yes."

"Aye," he said and nodded his head. "Just expose yer pecker to her. That's what I do. Works like a dream."

"You're serious?"

"No, I'm Upton," he replied, confused.

Nodding, I pondered his suggestion. It was definitely simple. However, flashing Tallulah seemed like a bad plan. I wasn't quite sure why, but I was going with my gut on this one.

"Interesting," I said. "While appealing in its simplicity, I feel it's a bit too bold a move at this juncture."

"Didn't understand a word of that, Captain," Upton said, squinting in confusion.

"That's because yer a floundering, barrel bellied son of a sea hound," Bonar grunted in disgust, backhanding Upton and sending him sprawling onto the deck. "Ya never show yer pecker until after ye has written the letter of love and serenaded the siren."

"Go on," I instructed Bonar. This plan had more merit, although I was tone deaf and had terrible penmanship.

"Ye need to pen the words of love and describe her knockers with flowery words. After ye have waxed poetic about her lady bits, ye will then need to sing a love song. Personally, I enjoy warbling the tunes of Whitesnake or Air Supply."

"So I just describe her bosom and list off a few flowers?" I inquired.

"Aye," Bonar said. "And I'd include comparing her arse to something ye admire."

"Like aged rum or horse racing?" I questioned, wanting to get all the correct information.

"Aye," Bonar replied. "I'd be happy to write yer love letter for ye, Captain."

"You would do that for me?" I asked, humbled by the offer. As I wasn't close to my family, these arses had become like brothers to me over the centuries.

"I would die for ye, Captain," Bonar replied. "I can write ye a love letter. Do ye happen to know any Whitesnake tunes?"

"No, I don't," I replied a bit worried. "However, I do know a few nursery rhymes."

Bonar wrinkled his brow and silently debated the merits of me singing Three Blind Mice, or else he was constipated. I wasn't sure, so I waited patiently.

"T'will be fine," he announced with the authority of a Pirate who had wooed many a floozy. "Sing soft and in her ear. Gets the wenches quite randy."

"Will do," I said, feeling more confident. I'd known none of these handy wooing techniques. This was going to be easier than I'd originally thought. I would read the love letter, then sing Three Blind Mice, and then reveal my pecker. Simple.

Thornycraft raised his good hand and waited his turn.

"Yes, matey?" I said.

"Captain, may I be so bold to offer ye one more piece of advice," he asked.

"Absolutely," I said.

"Ye should make her a nice meal and light a few candles."

"Why would I do that if I read the plagiarized love letter, sing, and show her my Johnson?" I asked. It was now getting complicated. And Thornycraft was missing most of his fingers, which disqualified him from having expertise in the lady department. If he couldn't keep his digits, how in the Seven Seas could he woo a wench?

"Because ye love the lass," he replied. "If ye love her, ye should feed her. Me mum says so. Also, yer supposed to ask her questions about herself."

"Can I talk about me?" I asked. I was my favorite subject.

"Of course," Thornycraft assured me. "But make sure for each thing ye brag about yerself, ye ask her a question about herself. Dinner and conversation. Me mum knows all."

"You still talk to your mum?" I asked, scanning the deck of the ship to see if my own mum was watching over me like my drunken sot of a father had warned. If the stalker was here, she hid herself well. Letting my chin drop to my chest, I sighed. Fate had been cruel. I could have used my mum's advice at the moment.

"Aye. I Skype with her every third Wednesday. She's a pain in me arse, but I love her," Thornycraft admitted.

"The thieving peg-legged shite has a fine point. Me mum would say the same—love note, song, tent pole reveal, food and conversation," Bonar agreed. "Just stay away from the beans. Can get a bit awkward."

"I feel you," I said, nodding my head and silently thanking Poseidon for sending me such brilliant men even if the green-haired bastard wouldn't tell me who my mother was. "All right then, get to work men. I'll be bringing my mate back to the ship for dinner. And keep an eye out for the Sea Hags."

"Aye, Captain," they said in unison.

"Does anyone know how to cook?" I asked as an afterthought. Normally, we just opened cans and dumped the contents on a plate. Somehow that didn't seem like the best idea to impress Tallulah.

"Nay, but it can't be that hard," Upton said. "I'll catch some fish and toss them in a pot."

"Works for me," I said. "Thornycraft, go ashore and invite

Tallulah to dinner. Tell her I've come up with a new strategy on how to take down the Hags."

"Aye, Captain, very crafty," Thornycraft said and then dove over the rail into the ocean. "What time?" he called out from the crashing waves.

"Six o'clock," I replied looking to the sun to gauge the time. Six o'clock would give me two hours to prepare. Perfect. "Bonar, get started on the letter of love. Upton, go catch some fish. I have a wench to woo."

Life was good and I was winning.

I loved winning.

9

TALLULAH

"WHAT WILL YOU WEAR?" MADISON ASKED AS SHE FLOPPED DOWN on my bed and began sorting through my choices.

My pretty room looked like a cyclone had blown through. Clothes were everywhere and my sumptuous lavender silk quilt had been carelessly tossed over the seashell headboard. Jeweled flip-flops littered the floor and a few bikini tops were hanging from the sparkling crystal chandelier. It was a hot mess —just like me at the moment.

"It doesn't matter what I wear," I said as butterflies danced in my stomach. "Pirate Doug is a gaping ass. We're going to discuss the Hags and how to get rid of them—that's all."

"Thought you already did that on the beach," Misty pointed out with a wide grin as she settled herself next to Madison.

"We did," I said and then groaned. "Do you think he assumes this is a date?"

"Well, he *is* an ass so *ass*uming is right up his alley," Ariel said with a giggle, entering the room with a clean and groomed Wally on her shoulder. "And apparently, he *ass*umes that you're his mate."

"He is *not* my mate," I insisted. "Can you imagine being tied to that... *thing*... for eternity?"

"That *thing* looks pretty impressive if his crotch rocket protector is anything to go by," Misty said shaking her head and trying not to laugh.

"Look," I said, pacing the room in a slight panic. "Pirate Doug is all sorts of pretty to look at and he's hung like a horse, but he's a thieving, untrustworthy jackhole too. He stole all of our gold coins for the love of everything fishy."

"This is true," Ariel said. "However, you haven't been this affected by a man in I don't know how long."

"A century," Madison stated.

"Yep," Misty agreed. "You haven't been interested in anyone since that sticky-fingered bastard was here a hundred years ago."

"Not true," I snapped, lying through my teeth. "And even if it was true, what exactly does that say about me and my taste in men?"

"Umm...well..." Ariel stuttered, biting back her smile. "It says you have shitty taste in men, but to be fair we all kind of go for the bad boys. Ol' Pirate Dud is particularly bad, but he is hotter than lava in an undersea volcano."

"I can't," I said on a long sigh. "He'll make my life hell and I'll have to kill him—which would be difficult and messy."

"Not to mention he's the son of Poseidon and heir to the throne," Madison reminded me.

"And there's *that*," I hissed. "That randy son of a bitch would never keep his bits in his pants if he becomes the God of the Sea. I'd have to castrate him weekly. Not my idea of a good time."

"But what if he was faithful?" Ariel asked.

"And what if great whites could fly?" I shot back.

"Have you seen Sharknado?" Ariel questioned.

"No. Why?"

"No reason," Ariel replied with a smirk. "I'm just saying as much of a doucheroll as he is, he might actually be your mate and once you're mated, his Johnson will only work for you."

"And he's hot," Madison pointed out as she pulled a shimmering gold bikini top and a matching sarong from the pile.

"There are plenty of attractive men that don't find robbing you blind amusing," I pointed out.

"Yep," Misty conceded. "Let's make a pro and con list."

"Let's not," I said. "I can already tell you Pirate Slug will not come out of it well."

"You chicken?" Misty challenged with a gleam in her eyes.

"Are you a butthole?" I growled.

"Yep," she replied with a laugh.

Ignoring my grumpy mood, Misty snapped her fingers and produced the shell and jewel- encrusted book we always used to make our most important decisions. Our dear sweet Mother had given it to us before she died many centuries ago. Even though the book was ancient, its magic was strong. It was still as sturdy and lovely as the day it was given to us.

"Pirate Doug doesn't deserve to be in the book," I said, getting nervous. What the hell was I going to do if the idiot came out on the pro side?

"All big decisions need the book," Madison said as she cradled Wally in her arms and cooed at her.

"Even manwhores deserve a chance, hooker," Wally squawked.

"What?" I asked, narrowing my eyes at the bird. "What did you say, Wally?"

"It's not Wally, wench," the bird said with an eye roll. "The dumbarse can't seem to remember my moniker—although that's not surprising considering it's not my real name."

"What is your real name?" Misty asked, clearly ignoring the fact that the foul-mouthed bird had called me a hooker.

"Promise not to tell?" Not-Wally questioned as she hopped to the bed and examined the pile of clothing.

"Promise," we said in unison.

"It's Janet," she announced.

I bit down hard on my lips so I wouldn't laugh. She was so not a Janet.

"Like *'Damn it, Janet. I love you'?*" Ariel asked in all seriousness.

"Is that hooker right in the head?" Janet asked.

"No. She watches a lot of movies. You'll have to excuse her," I said with a laugh.

"No worries," Janet chirped as she kicked all of the ensembles off the bed except the gold one. "I've been living on that damned ship for fifty years. I'm used to idiocy that you wouldn't believe."

I stared at the parrot for a long moment. I was fairly sure she wasn't a parrot at all, but it wasn't exactly my place to point that out. If Pirate Doug's fear of her was accurate, I would guess she could be quite violent.

Or maybe she loved Doug...

I didn't like the little green monster that popped into my head and longed to deck the innocent bird. I didn't like it at all. What the hell was wrong with me?

"So," I said, picking up the pile of clothes off the floor so I didn't have my hands free to de-wing Janet. "How long have you known Pirate Doug?"

Janet gazed back at me. I could swear she was grinning and could read my mind. Shit.

"Since the day the little bastard was born," she replied.

"So you're aware that he's less than stellar in the morals, brains and manners department," I snapped.

"He's an epic ass, but I love the little shit. Can't help it," Janet replied as she flew over to me and got in my personal space. "Does that bother you, girlie?"

She was screwing with me. I knew it. She knew it and my sisters knew it. Janet's minutes on Earth were numbered.

"Are you in love with him?" she demanded.

"Are you?" I countered as my hair began to blow around my head and a lavender-scented wind kicked up blowing everything around my room willy-nilly.

The bird cackled and walloped me on the back of my head, sending me flying across my messy room.

"What the what?" I shouted as I got to my feet and prepared to rip the sack of feathers in half.

Raising my hands above my head, I was ready to off the obnoxious pet of the jackass who wanted to woo me. He didn't seem to like her much so I figured it was probably fine.

"Not so fast, hooker," Janet bellowed and then laughed like a loon. "You love him *and* you hate him. Wonderful."

"What are you idiots sniffing out there on that ship?" I demanded. The bird was as insane as her owner.

"Fish guts and farts," Janet cackled. "You're gonna have to make the boy work for it. I'd suggest a year for every gold coin he pilfered from you."

"Wait," I said, lowering my itchy trigger fingers and glaring at the bird. "You lost me. I thought you loved the jackhole."

"I do," she said and puffed out her scrawny chest. "But not the same way you do, hooker. That would be illegal."

"Care to be more specific?" I asked, narrowing my eyes at the smack talking feathered freak.

"Nope."

We silently eyed at each other for a minute and then I shrugged. "Doesn't matter. I don't want the thieving dolt."

"Liar, liar, bikini on fire," Janet crowed and flew around the room dropping bombs of turd everywhere. "I think the book will prove me right."

"Plug that sphincter or I'll plug it for you," I warned. "And trust me, it won't be pleasant."

"You're a violent little vixen," Janet squawked with approval. "You'll give me some spicy grandchildren."

Janet quit flying midair and dropped to the ground with a thud. She was as shocked by her admission as I was.

"Loose lips sink ships," I muttered with a grin.

I had her. She was about to spill her guts or I was going to bust her pooping ass.

"Shite," she groaned and slapped herself on the head with her wing. "Didn't mean to say that."

"Start talking, bird, or you're gonna have some explaining to do to your *son*," I threatened.

"Fine. What do you want to know?" Janet huffed and pooped in protest.

"Everything. I want to know everything."

10

PIRATE DOUG

"WHAT'S THAT SMELL?" TALLULAH ASKED, WRINKLING HER NOSE and trying not to gag.

I sniffed the air in alarm and shook my head to clear it. My brain wasn't functioning on all cylinders due to the mouthwatering scraps of material Tallulah had chosen to wear. The dinghy ride over had been a monstrous challenge.

Keeping my hands to myself had taken all the self-control I had—not that I had much to begin with. I'd accidentally rowed in circles for thirty minutes before I could figure out how to maneuver the small craft back to the ship. Thankfully my Johnson-induced lack of coordination seemed to amuse my Mermaid.

Now finally back on the ship, I was panicked that something had gone awry in my absence. Glancing around, I tried to sniff out the location of the heinous aroma. Was it Bonar? Or Thornycraft? Or Upton? Or me? No. We might be Pirates, but our hygiene was impeccable. Besides, my crew wasn't even on the ship of the moment. They were standing watch over the isle and keeping an eye out for the Hags.

At least forty Tiki torches were blazing and an inviting array of stolen chaise lounges had been placed next to a perfectly set pilfered table for two. The letter of love was in my pocket and I'd warmed up my voice before I'd retrieved my lady. Upton did suffer a slight ear bleed due to my singing but healed up quite nicely. My breeches were loose fitting for easy removal to reveal my pecker and dinner was on the fire.

I'd also come up with something on my own. This was risky, but I felt that a personal touch would be prudent to my wooing. It was something unheard of for me, but desperate times called untried measures.

"Sweet shark in a leisure suit," I gasped out and swallowed the bile rising in my throat. What in the hell had Upton chosen to cook for dinner? It smelled like a pot of arse.

"Did something die?" Tallulah inquired, pinching her nose shut with her slim fingers.

"No. But someone is about to," I muttered, rushing over to the kettle of boiling butts.

Peeking inside, I almost heaved. It was full of fish, seaweed, beans, onions, eggs and pickles. Upton had clearly lied about his cooking prowess. I'd kick his arse later. This was a catastrophe. Picking up the searing hot pot with my bare hands, I heaved the shite-smelling concoction over the railing and then tried to play it off.

"Apparently, the caterer was drunk," I said and then wondered how she would feel about a few cans of tuna and some day old bread.

"That's fine, I'm not really hungry," Tallulah said, glancing around the deck. "Aren't you concerned about setting your ship ablaze?"

She had a fine point, but Thornycraft's mum had said candles were important. Of course, I'd upped the ante by choosing enormous torches, but my motto was always go big or go home. Although an inferno would really put a crimp in my plans...

"Not at all," I lied, praying to Poseidon that we didn't end up crispy. "I enjoy a little danger. Don't you?"

"Umm... sure," she said with a laugh. "I'm here aren't I?"

"That you are," I bellowed and led her to the arrangement of shoplifted furniture.

Seating her with a flourish, I realized I was terrified. Never before had a hooker made me feel so unsure about my man skills. Well, that wasn't exactly true...

Only one other time had I felt so at a loss. It was a hundred years ago and it was caused by the very same woman sitting before me now. But instead of trying to figure out the unfamiliar feelings at the time, I'd absconded with all of her booty and tried to put her out of my mind. Clearly, I'd failed and now I was afraid I was failing again.

Attempting to serve her a pot of stinky arse for dinner wasn't a good start.

"So tell me about yourself," I said looking down at my hand. I'd had the forethought to write a few conversation starters on my palm. "Do you recycle?"

"What?" Tallulah asked, squinting at me strangely.

"Sorry, wrong question," I replied hastily. Thornycraft was an arsehole. His suggestion that I use a textbook to procure my questions from was going to bite me in my nards. "What I meant was, how do you feel about new math?"

The Mermaid simply stared at me with her mouth slightly open.

"Whoops," I shouted, hoping my sheer volume might distract from the appalling questions I'd chosen. "Shall I reveal my Johnson now, sing, or read you the letter of love?"

Narrowing her gorgeous lavender eyes, Tallulah bit back what I was certain was laughter. This was not supposed to be a fucking comedy routine. I was beginning to sweat and was mentally planning to make my crew walk the plank very shortly. Their advice was bullshit.

"Doug?" Tallulah questioned. "What's going on here?"

Sighing dramatically and dropping into the seat next to her, I let my head fall to my hands. "I'm trying to woo you," I muttered. "Is it working?"

"Actually, it kind of is," she said with a giggle.

Peeking over at her through splayed fingers, I grinned. "I'm not used to this."

"Clearly," she said with a giggle. "Why are you doing it?"

"You called me Doug," I replied truthfully, wondering if I should check my palm for another question.

"That's your name."

"Yes, well... no one calls me *Doug*. I don't allow it, but when you did it, I liked it. At first, I thought the feeling was due to the legumes I'd eaten earlier, but it wasn't. You're the one meant for me," I said, laying it all out on the table.

"Hmm," she replied non-committedly. "Interesting. So what is this letter of love?"

Her scent was full of lust and I became hopeful. Maybe I hadn't ruined everything... yet. Pulling the parchment paper from my pocket, I stood tall and proud. Bonar's penmanship was iffy, but I could make out most of it.

"Hooker of my dreams—my future mate," I started. "Your knockers are like a marathon of Chuck Norris movies and your breath doesn't stink. The thought of your melons suffocating me is more appealing than getting snockered at Willie's Whiskey Bar in the Grand Caymans where there are seventy-two warrants out for my arrest. I dream of riding you like a horse in the Kentucky Derby and then de-thorning all the roses in the winners circle floral arrangement and doing you atop them—in public—until neither of us can walk."

I was wildly unsure if this was working, but the mention of both horse racing and flowers were required elements. This had to be a good thing. Tallulah's expression was either one of shock, disgust, or awe. It was anyone's guess, but I chose to go with awe.

Continuing, I raised my volume so she would be more impressed. It would also warm her ears up for my singing. "Daisies, tulips, marigolds and carnations," I bellowed. That wasn't on the note, but listing off flowers was important. It was a fine thing I had an excellent memory for details. "Your arse is lovelier than the hot dogs sold at Wrigley Field during a doubleheader and I'd enjoy biting it. Seeing you greased up like a watermelon at a Fourth of July..."

"Umm, you should probably stop right there," Tallulah insisted loudly with an enormous eye roll that didn't bode well for my cause. Fucking Bonar.

"It's not working?"

"No. No it's not. Did you write that crap?" she asked, standing up to leave.

Tossing the letter of love behind me, I frantically ripped off my pants and revealed my Johnson. "I didn't write it," I swore as I did a few vocal warm-ups. "Three blind mice," I sang as she winced in pain.

"Enough," she shouted with a squeal of laughter. "You're out of your mind."

"Your point?" I asked, completely confused. What did that have to do with anything?

"Was *any* of this your idea?" she questioned.

I considered lying for a brief moment but decided against it. I sucked at this wooing shit. "No," I admitted, putting my breeches back on. "I had one idea of my own, but now I'm afraid to try it."

Tallulah eyed me cautiously and sat back down. "Try it. Let's see how well you do on your own, Pirate."

It was a risk, but I didn't have anything else up my sleeves.

"Do you promise not to behead me, Mermaid?" I inquired, thinking that would be a horrible way to end the evening.

"Yes, but the rest of your appendages are fair game," she informed me with a crooked smile that made me want to fall at her feet and worship her for the rest of time.

"It's in my quarters," I told her sheepishly. "Not that I don't dream of having you in my cabin, but my surprise is truly in there."

"Are you trying to seduce me, Pirate?"

"Most definitely, Mermaid. However, I do have a gift of sorts for you."

She paused for only a moment and then stood. "Lead me to your quarters, *Doug*. I want my surprise."

Sweeter words had never been spoken.

11

TALLULAH

HE WAS A LYING SACK OF CRAP, BUT I'D KNOWN THIS FROM DAY one. It clearly hadn't stopped me from falling under his ridiculous spell a hundred years ago and it wasn't going to stop me now. I wanted him as much as he wanted me and his attempts at wooing me—however appalling—were kind of cute. After a long conversation with Janet, I had a new understanding of the idiot I was drawn to.

He'd been turned into a Vampire as a child and Janet had been forced by the gods to leave him to fend for himself. As he was to ascend to his father's throne someday, this was the way it was done. While Poseidon had been allowed to monitor Doug's growth, his mother was forbidden to intervene. It was all sexist bullshit, and if I actually mated with the sexy dolt, I was going to have a few choice words with the gods as to how I was going to raise my children. They could kiss my Mermaid ass before I let them take away my baby. My sisters meant the world to me. I couldn't even imagine what I would feel for my very own child.

Janet had caught Apollo in a very compromising position

about fifty years ago and was finally able to watch over her son due to a fabulous blackmail scheme. However, she wasn't supposed to tell him who she was and that was where I was supposed to come in when the time was right. Whether Pirate Doug could convince me that I was truly his mate or not, I would still tell him about his mother. Family was important. I'd be lost without my sisters.

"It's surprisingly clean in here," I commented as we made our way down a narrow hallway towards his room.

"I think Jolly cleans when we're not looking," Doug explained. "Speaking of Qually… has she attacked anyone yet? She's a rather violent flying fucker."

"Umm, no not exactly attacked," I said, wondering if the time was right. Nope. I wanted to get laid and telling a man his long lost mother was a foulmouthed parrot wasn't conducive to foreplay.

"If you like her, you can have her," he offered. "I've tried to lose the damned shitter for fifty years. She just keeps coming back."

"I think you might like her if you'd give her a chance," I said, trying to help old Janet out.

Pirate Doug's laugh shot all through me. It was delightful to see him happy.

"I hate her feathered arse, but I'd probably miss the turd-dropping She-Devil if she was gone," he admitted and stopped in front of a closed door with pictures of Chuck Norris taped all over it.

Deciding not to comment that the door to his quarters should belong to a fourth grade human boy, I waited. I had to admit I was slightly terrified of what was behind the door if the love letter and the song were anything to go by.

"You ready?" he asked with a panty-melting grin that made my lady bits perk up.

"Nope, but that's never stopped me before," I replied.

He held open the door and grinned like a fool. It was all I could do not to tackle him and kiss him silly. I really needed my head examined. Slowly, I entered his room. With his maturity level as *high* as it was, I couldn't be sure it wasn't booby-trapped. It wasn't. Not even a little bit.

My breath caught in my throat and I turned to gape at him.

"Is that what I think it is?" I whispered.

"It is," he said, scrunching his nose in embarrassment. "I never spent it and I never knew why until now. It's been underneath my bed for a hundred years."

The chest was exactly as I remembered it—dark polished wood with colorful seashells embedded in it. It was exquisite. My sisters and I had carved our names in the treasure chest as little Mermaids and our Mother had as well.

"Is there anything in it?" I asked as I approached treasure chest.

"Every last gold coin," he promised. "I'd like to return it to you—not that it makes it okay that I pilfered it in the first place, but..."

He was a Pirate—a sticky fingered, thieving swashbuckler. It was against Pirate code to repay a debt. Everyone knew this. It was definitely crappy that he stole it, but it was life-changing for him to return it. And to think he'd kept it safe under his bed for a century.

The Pirate was all kinds of awful, but I wanted him more than I wanted to swim in the ocean. Oh, I knew I'd want to dismember him on a regular basis, but life without the nardhole seemed hopelessly empty. Not that I was about to come clean about my feelings just yet.

"Okay. You can woo me," I blurted out without thinking.

"I can?" he asked with huge eyes and a wide grin.

"Yes," I said with an eye roll. "However, it's going to take a *very long* time for you to succeed."

"Interesting," he said, kicking his cabin door shut and

approaching me like I was prey. "Is nookie off limits during the wooing period?"

"What if I said it was?" I demanded, crossing my arms over my chest and making sure that I was pushing my girls up high.

Doug's knees buckled and it was all I could do not to jump him. Watching as he tried to form words while his eyes were glued to my chest was delightful.

"Well, umm… if those are the rules, I guess I could masturbate frequently," he stuttered.

"You would do that for me?" I purred, sitting down on his enormous bed and crossing my legs so my sarong proved that I'd forgotten my panties—on purpose.

"Would you watch?" he choked out.

"Doug?"

"Tallulah?" he replied now bent over at the waist and clearly in pain.

"Nookie is *not* off the table."

"Are you serious?" he wheezed, looking ridiculously hopeful.

"No, I'm Tallulah," I said with a laugh. "Take off your clothes, Pirate. I want to see if you're still worth it."

It the blink of an eye my Pirate was completely naked. I lost the power of speech for a moment as I gaped at his sheer muscular beauty. Over six feet of beautifully muscled, gorgeous man. And his bits were not bitty at all.

"I've dreamt of you for a hundred years," Doug said softly as he crossed the room.

Gone was the bumbling idiot and in his place was the greatest lover of the Seven Seas—and he was all mine.

"Have you?" I asked as I slowly removed my shimmering gold bikini top and let it fall to the floor. "What happened in these dreams?"

His chuckle sent a zing of pleasure right to my girlie parts and I quickly dispensed of my sarong. A fragrant ocean breeze blew through the open window and the glow of the moon made his beauty appear otherworldly.

"Well," he admitted with a sexy crooked smirk. "The end of the dream is usually rather violent."

"How so?" I inquired as I scooted back on the bed and ran my hands suggestively down my body.

Doug's eyes hooded and began to glow. His sexy Vampire fangs appeared and I shuddered in delight with memories of what he could do with those sharp canines.

"It's fabulous until you remove my Johnson."

My laugh was loud and he grinned as he stopped at the edge of the bed and stared at me.

"You are exquisite, Tallulah—beautiful and strong. And your knockers—your knockers are a work of art."

His choice of words was a little off putting, but the sentiment was very clear. He could have called my girls hooters and I wouldn't have cared.

"You're not so bad yourself," I said and crooked my finger at him to join me on his bed.

"I know. My tallywacker is outstanding," he agreed as he jumped on the bed and pressed his body against mine.

His skin was hot and his scent was delicious. I hadn't felt this free and happy in so long. We were definitely going to have to discuss the way he made his living, but I had an idea. Actually Janet had come up with it, but it was all kinds of brilliant.

"That depends on what you can do with your tallywacker," I pointed out as I ran my hands over his chest and pressed my lips to his neck.

"You're like an addiction," he growled as he scraped my aching breast with his fangs sending pleasure through my body that I'd forgotten I could have. "An addiction I will never kick."

"I certainly hope not," I gasped out as he nipped and licked his way down my needy body. "Oh and by the way… I'll make your dream a reality if you so much as look at another woman."

"You would?" he asked, looking up at me with delight.

"I would," I confirmed with a giggle.

"And I shall repay the compliment," Doug announced as his fingers found the spot that made my back arch with desire and a moan fly from my lips. "I shall behead any man that makes a play for you and will chain you to my bed for eternity if you ever try to leave me."

"Gods, that's so hot," I squealed as his mouth replaced his fingers and stars shot across my vision. "And if you ever try to leave me again, I'll remove your Johnson with a dull butter knife."

His chuckle against my most private parts sent me into an orgasm that ripped through me like a shot from a pistol.

"I believe you already threatened to remove my jolly roger if I looked at another," he replied and then went back to work on making me orgasm again.

"Right," I gasped out. "You're correct. I guess I would shove your balls down your throat then."

"Excellent," he shouted and moved up my body so quickly I didn't even see him move. "You are a violent goddess and you are mine."

"You still have to woo me for a few decades," I reminded him as my hands found his very hard and very large treasure.

"Will do," he choked out on a hiss of lust. "I shall work hard for your hand."

"You're very hard *in* my hand right now," I replied with a giggle as I stroked the rock hard evidence of his desire and bit at his full lips.

"Do you think we should do something about that?" he whispered in my ear as his hips rocked into my hand.

"I could think of a few things we could do to make you feel better."

"Show me," he begged hoarsely against my lips.

And I did.

Opening my legs and guiding the Pirate of my dreams to where I wanted him to be was the scariest and most exhilarating thing I'd done in a century. As his body became one with mine all thoughts of Sea Hags and failing tourist business disappeared. What I was feeling was right and perfect and I deserved it.

"I can't go slow," Doug growled as he jerked his hips forward and buried himself to the hilt inside me. "I want you too much. I promise I'll go slow on the tenth time."

"You can do it ten times?" I asked on a half laugh-half moan as he filled me and sent mini-orgasms shuddering through me.

"I'm Pirate Doug, the greatest Vampire Pirate lover of the Seven Seas," he bragged as he began to move. "You are Tallulah of the Mystical Island Pod—the sexiest damned wench in the world and you're mine. I can go twelve times tonight."

"Go for it, Pirate," I challenged as I writhed underneath him and met each strong thrust with joyous abandon.

And he did.

And he was correct... almost.

We did it thirteen times.

And it was fucking fabulous—pun intended.

"THAT WAS..." DOUG SAID DREAMILY, HOLDING ME CLOSE WHILE he searched for the right words.

"Mind blowing, wonderful and perfect," I replied quickly before he could destroy the moment by comparing me to a horse or a greased watermelon.

"I want you to be my mate," he whispered.

The moonlight bathed us in her magical glow and I realized that I wanted the very same thing, but he was still going to have to work for it.

"You're going to have to make it right with my sisters," I told him as I traced little circles on his lightly haired chest. "My family is very important to me."

Doug sighed and kissed the top of my head. "I wouldn't know about that. I barely know my nine hundred and twenty siblings and my Pappy is an arse with an alarming hairdo."

"And your mother?" I asked.

"The wench didn't want me," he said, shrugging his wide shoulders. "Supposedly, the hooker has been spying on me for a while, but if she cared for me she would show her face."

I held my breath for a long moment and then slowly let it out.

"Can I tell you a story?" I asked.

"A bedtime story?" Doug questioned, sounding like a lost little boy.

"Umm... kind of. You have to promise me you won't be mad."

Doug sat up and glared at me. "Are you already promised to someone else?" he growled as his eyes began to glow with fury.

"No. No, hold your seahorses," I insisted quickly before he blew up the ship with both of us on it. "I am promised to no one. And I make my own decisions—always. We are not living in the dark ages anymore."

"Thank the gods for that," he muttered, calming down and pulling me back into his strong arms. "So is this a nice story?"

"Depends."

"Like the adult diaper?" he questioned.

"Umm... no," I said with a giggle. "Why don't you just listen and decide for yourself."

"I can do that," he said, playing with my long lavender locks. "As long as you don't leave me or yank my Johnson off everything will be okay."

I certainly hoped so...

12
_____

PIRATE DOUG

"So tell me," I said, staring daggers at Wally *aka* Janet *aka* my mother. "Do you actually believe crapping on your son's head for half a century is good parenting?"

"Your behavior merited a few shits," she replied with a grin.

While Wally had a valid point, her method left much to be desired. I would *never* poop on my child's head—not that I had a child or even a pet. Wally clearly didn't count anymore. I planned on siring at least twenty or thirty-two children but I hadn't sprung that bit of news on Tallulah yet. I was waiting until the time was right and I had developed an impenetrable Johnson protector.

The morning had dawned bright and sunny—the exact opposite of my mood. It had taken Tallulah telling me the story twelve times before I realized it was a non-fiction tale. So now, slathered in an absurd amount of sunscreen, I was facing my newest issue head on.

Everyone had assembled on the beach to witness the reunion—or possibly to make sure I didn't throw a shit fit that blew the island off the map of the Bermuda Triangle. Tallulah and her sisters flanked my *mother* and my men stood by me. The rest of the gaggle of colorful swimming hookers dotted the beach and watched with interest. It was clear they had no clue what was going on, but Mermaids were nosy wenches.

I knew Tallulah was on my side, but as I was still in the process of wooing her, her placement was appropriate. Plus, I was fairly sure her sisters didn't like me yet. Hopefully, the return of the booty and the sheer amount of orgasms I'd given their sister would sway them. However, the most bizarre fact was that Wally was no longer a parrot—and I wasn't quite sure how I felt about that.

The horrible woman looked just like me or rather, I looked like her. Since I enjoyed staring at myself, it was fascinating to stare at a female version of me. However, I was pissed at the old bag and didn't have the time to admire how good I would look with knockers.

Not to mention how odd it was seeing Wally as a person. Her shift from parrot to human was alarming. Upton had puked. I wasn't sure if it was because he was remembering the heinous or embarrassing misdeeds he had done in front of my *mother* over the years or if he was simply grossed out. There was no way in the Seven Seas I would call her Mother. Hell, I wasn't sure I could call her Janet either. It was going to be Wally for the time being.

"A few, Wally?" I demanded. "You call pooping on my head numerous times a day for fifty fucking years… a *few*?"

"Fine," she said with a shrug. "I'm a little sorry."

"Define *a little*," I snapped.

Wally laughed and winked at me. I liked it, but I still glared at the old wench. It wouldn't do at all to tackle her and hug her. She had a tremendous amount of questions to answer.

"I'm very sorry for shitting on you. I really wanted to take you over my knee and beat your arse for some of the things you've done over the last few decades. And as that was not a possibility, I figured dropping stinkies on your head would have to suffice," she explained.

"Makes sense to me," Bonar chimed in.

"Did *your* mother take dumps on *your* head?" I demanded of my turncoat crew member.

"Umm... not that I recall," Bonar admitted. "But I'm sure the landlubbin' old cow would have if she could."

"You're not helping," I ground out through clenched teeth.

"Aye," he nodded. "My bad, Captain."

"I should say so," I muttered and tried to think of all the things I wanted to ask the loose sphinctered wench.

"Doug," Wally started.

"Pirate Doug," I corrected her. She would have to earn calling me Doug.

"*Pirate Doug*," she amended with a little grin. "I've been living as a fucking bird for fifty years. I gave up my demi-goddess status—complete with wardrobe, an all you can eat buffet and ballroom dancing lessons—for my son. The word arse is now part of my vocabulary thanks to you."

"You're welcome," I replied. It wouldn't kill me to be polite.

"No, I was being... never mind," Wally said with an outstanding eye roll that should have caused her eyes to get stuck in the back of her head.

It was very impressive.

"I've cleaned up after you and your messy idiots for half a century. You imbeciles are disgusting. I would think that should count for something. Don't you?"

"Is that a trick question?" I inquired, squinting at her. "And will you be dropping turds all over the place as a human?"

"Umm, no and no," she answered, shaking her head. "I wanted to be near you and I wasn't permitted to reveal myself."

"So you *like* me?" I asked, doing my best to sound nonchalant.

"Not particularly," she admitted with a chuckle. "But I do love you. You have no clue how awful it is to be a parrot."

"It sucked arse?" I inquired.

"It sucked arse," she confirmed.

I paced the sand in a zig-zag path to avoid the toe pinching sand crabs. Those little arseholes were vicious.

What to do...

I had wanted a mother my entire life and here she was. Tallulah loved her family. My soon to be mate valued her family greatly. Hmmm, could I knock a few decades off the wooing process if I let Wally into my life?

Could I love this crapping wench named Janet who'd lived as a bag of feathers for fifty years just to be near me?

Could she be trusted not to poop all over my ship? Would my mother be willing to wear adult diapers until she could prove that she wasn't a shitting risk?

So many things to consider.

"Captain?" Bonar interrupted my jumbled thoughts.

"Little busy here thinking," I said.

"Aye, but ye might have a problem," he informed me.

"I already know that," I huffed. "Wally is my *mother*."

"Ye has another problem too," Upton chimed in, still pale from losing his cookies.

"Is it more important than literally being defecated on by a parental unit?" I questioned, annoyed.

"Depends," Bonar said.

"Yes, yes, I've already thought of that," I replied, impressed that my man had pondered making my mother wear diapers too. "We'll have to raid a Target to supply ourselves."

"Aye, Captain," Bonar replied looking incredibly confused. "But I was talking about yonder ship being on fire."

Quickly scanning the horizon I spied my favorite ship

ablaze atop the water, I stomped my foot and caused a large crater in the beach. How in the hell was I supposed to sail the Seven Seas and pilfer my way around the world without my favorite ship? "Son of a beach," I bellowed. "How did that happen?"

"Possibly the forty Tiki torches?" Tallulah volunteered, patting me on the back.

"Damn it," I griped and smacked my forehead. "I forgot to blow them out."

"Possibly or maybe not," Wally said, as she began to glow and grow in size.

My mother was now the size of a large freighter ship. It was amazing to see something that resembled me so enormous. However, it also meant she could kick my arse—not good.

Wally quickly shoved all of us behind her and roared out at the sea.

"Is it the fucking Kraken?" I shouted above her fury as I too began to glow.

"No," she said with relief as her body slowly went back to normal size.

"The Sea Hags?" Tallulah demanded as she got into a fighting stance alongside her sisters.

"No. No Hags in me sight yet," Thornycroft reported.

My gal was a killer. My roger grew jolly at the sight of her all glowly and vicious.

"Not now, you randy little shit," Wally snapped and walloped me in the back of the head sending me flying into my men. "You shall pay attention to the fucking matter at hand."

"You're kinda mean," I muttered. "You said it wasn't the Kraken and it's not the Hags, so I don't see a problem here."

Wally grunted in disgust and strode over to me, causing me to hide behind my idiots.

"You have been listening to your tallywhacker for far too

long. You are going to straighten up and fly right. You're going to find a new career and settle down."

"New career?" I asked suspiciously. "Define." I enjoyed my career and I was excellent at it.

"It *is* the Sea Hags!" Tallulah shouted and turned to the terrified Mermaids on the beach. "Run, hookers. Run."

The hookers not trained to fight scattered quickly leaving me, my men, Wally, Tallulah and her sisters to fight the smelly abominations headed our way. The flaming ship was the least of our problems now. There were at least twenty Hags in the distance, zooming toward the island. The stench was worse than the time we realized Bonar had given up showering for Lent. They were about five minutes from us and flying fast.

"Tallulah," I commanded. "Take your sisters and hide with the hookers."

"*What?*" she snapped and slapped her hands onto her shapely hips.

"I have found getting into your underpants is my new life's goal. If you're offed by a creature that can fuck itself, that could be a problem," I explained.

"I don't wear underpants," she shouted.

"I know. I was being polite." A huge grin pulled at my lips and my breeches grew painfully tight. Thankfully, I narrowly missed the left hook from Wally. My mother had been a pain in my arse as a bird and was equally as heinous as a person.

"It's kinda hot that he wants to protect you," Misty pointed out to her fuming sister.

"And kinda sexist pig-ish," Tallulah hissed and glared at me. "While the sentiment is weird and somewhat appreciated, I'll have a violent go at your Johnson if you ever tell me what to do again. This is *my* island and I will fight to the death to protect my people and my shitty tourist business. You feel me, jackhole?"

My eyes went wide and my breeches were now strangling

my Johnson. She was a rude, vicious work of art. And she was mine.

"I'll be *feeling* you in about an hour," I replied with a joyous laugh, proud of my bloodthirsty mate to be. "Who is the leader of this particular clusterfuck of Hags?"

"Bony Velma Dustface," Tallulah informed me with a shudder of disgust. "She's as mean as a snake and smells like New York City during a garbage strike in August."

"You have got to be shitting me," I yelled and slapped myself in the head.

"I shit you not," she replied. "Have you been in New York in August?"

"No, not that," I said with an eye roll. "Are you sure about the name of the leader? Could you be mistaken? Maybe it's Bony Velma Crustcase or possibly Bony Velma Rustrace?"

Of all the Sea Hags it had to be *Bony Velma Dustface*? Could today get much worse?

"It's Bony Velma *Dustface*. Is that a problem?" Tallulah demanded as her eyes narrowed. "Do you know her?"

"*Yesssss*, I know her."

"In the biblical sense?" she screeched in a fury while gagging.

"For the love of everything waterlogged," I bellowed, holding back my bile with effort. "Of course not. I would never poke my sister. That's disgusting."

Everyone froze and stared at me. When your Pappy couldn't keep his pecker in his pants, things like this were bound to happen. As one of nine hundred and twenty-one offspring, I was surprised I even knew Bony Velma was a relation. However, all of us knew Velma. Her stench and her temper were the stuff legends were made of.

"Bony Velma Dustface is your *sister*?" Tallulah asked, looking as shocked as I felt.

"Unfortunately yes," I admitted. "Haven't seen her in

almost five hundred years—never liked her much—very uncouth."

Again with the silence. While everyone was contemplating this smelly wrinkle, the Sea Hags were gaining ground.

"Wait a minute. I thought they multiplied by fornicating with themselves," Ariel said, wildly perplexed.

"Yes, that's nightmare-inducingly true," I confirmed. "My Pappy Poseidon gave them that *talent*—for lack of a more palatable word—due to the odiferous fact that no one wanted to play hide the salami with them. Apparently in a drunken stupor—common state for my Pappy—he banged a Hag and poof... Bony Velma Dustface was born."

"Your father is a manwhore," Wally grunted in disgust.

"Accurate," I replied with a wince of embarrassment. I wasn't exactly innocent in that department, but I was changing my ways.

"You can't kill your *sister*," Tallulah announced.

"Says who?" I asked.

"Says me," she shot back.

"And why not?" I demanded, clueless to her reasoning.

"Because she's your *family*."

I pondered this for a brief moment. My father had green hair, an appalling taste in banjo music and a horrifying penchant for fathering offspring. My mother had crapped on my head for fifty years and my sister was a foul smelling creature that could reproduce solo. My *family* was slightly dysfunctional.

"Fine," I conceded, more so Tallulah wouldn't castrate me than actually agreeing with her. "Bonar can behead her."

"Aye," Bonar said with a thumbs up. "Ye wish is me command."

"Umm... no. Absolutely not," Tallulah said firmly. "We're going to find another way here."

"Good luck with that," Wally said, pointing to the furious Sea Hags fast approaching.

"I have an idea," Tallulah growled, stepping out in front of all of us. "Follow my lead."

"Poseidon, help us all," Wally muttered.

I couldn't have agreed more.

13

TALLULAH

I HAD NO IDEA WHAT I PLANNED TO DO, BUT LETTING DOUG KILL his sister was way off the list of options. Family was family no matter how smelly. I'd simply pull a strategy out of my rear end and pray to Poseidon it worked. Of course, we wouldn't be in this shit show if it wasn't for Poseidon and his overactive man tool, but that was neither here nor there at the moment.

"Surrender," Rickety Sheila Clotlegs screeched as she came to a halt in the air about fifty feet offshore and took in the warriors assembled on the beach.

"Not so fast, Hag," I shouted. "The rules for total destruction of tourist traps haven't been put in place yet."

Rickety Shelia growled and glared at me. "What are you babbling about, Mermaid?"

"Rule sixty-nine clearly states that in order to legally smack down on an island in the Bermuda Triangle, the leaders of both factions in the dispute must be present. If not, Poseidon will technically own the island and the rule breakers will be imprisoned for eternity in a typhoon filled with sharks, piranhas and massive deodorant sticks."

"Seriously?" Doug whispered, shocked.

Thankfully Janet whacked his head so I didn't have to.

"*Deodorant* you say?" Rickety Shelia questioned with a terrified shudder.

"Deodorant," I confirmed. "Cocoa Kiss, Passion Paradise and Orchid Surprise."

The shrieks of terror from the Sea Hags helped me hatch my plan. It was weird and had a whole lot of holes in it, but it might work.

The Sea Hags clustered up and began muttering frantically with each other. Obviously in disagreement, they beat the living snot out of each other while we looked on in shock. Their number went from twenty down to six. Not because they offed each other, but because the smelly idiots were terrified of deodorant and deserted. I was pretty sure that Rickety Shelia wanted to fly away as well, but she held her ground.

"You drive a vicious bargain, Tallulah of the Mystical Island Pod," she hissed. "But we shall abide by the rules—for now. Are you packing deodorant sticks?"

"We are unarmed at the moment," I replied, trying not to laugh. "However, the Mermaids you displaced from their islands are hidden in the sand dunes and armed with not only deodorant sticks but also aerosol spray cans."

"That's very bad for the environment," Rickety Shelia pointed out.

"Yep," I agreed, biting back my grin with effort. "Desperate times call for environmentally unsound measures."

"I see," she said.

"And the hookers are packing shampoo," Ariel informed the increasingly pale Hags.

"Along with hair brushes, tweezers and leg hair removal cream," Misty threatened.

"And toothbrushes!" Madison shouted.

"Diabolical," a Sea Hag from behind Rickety Shelia Clotlegs bellowed. "You creatures are evil."

"Show yourself, Bony Velma Dustface," I demanded. "I know that's you. Come out from behind your stank ass minions and stop acting like a weenie."

And she did.

And we all gasped and plugged our noses.

I'd never actually laid eyes on the rank leader of the Sea Hags. She usually sent her minions—but not today. The resemblance to Pirate Doug was uncanny—that is if Doug was an unkempt, greenish, atrociously odiferous woman with no teeth.

"State your position, evil Mermaid," Bony Velma grunted, flying in tight circles as her Hags hovered around her. "We have an hour before *The Price Is Right* comes on and I didn't record it."

"I love The *Price Is Right*," Doug mumbled.

Thankfully Janet was still within smacking distance of her son and sent him flying. The deodorant was an excellent ploy, but I had an ace in the hole... or I hoped I did. It would knock years off the penance I'd sentenced Doug to, but I didn't care. I loved the bumbling fool and I was ready to let the world know. I might live to regret my rash action, but regret was for jellyfish. I was not a jellyfish. I was a Mermaid with a tourist business and a tremendous number of hookers to protect.

"I would like to introduce you to my mate," I shouted at Bony Velma.

"*What?* Where is he? I'll kill him," Doug roared as he picked himself up off the sand. His fangs had dropped and his eyes glowed menacingly.

His intelligence level and inability to go with the flow were going to get him an ass kicking from me shortly, but that would have to wait. We needed to live through the next few minutes.

"You are," I hissed as I grabbed him by the collar of his flowy Pirate shirt and jerked him up.

"I am?" he asked, quite pleased. "I thought you were still

thinking about it. What made you decide? The size of my trouser snake?"

"Shut your cakehole and smile or you'll have to regrow your trouser snake," I hissed under my breath.

"Roger that," he replied with a wide and adorable grin.

I really needed my head checked.

"Doug?" Bony Velma Dustface questioned, aghast. "Is that you?"

"*Pirate Doug,*" he corrected her.

"My bad," she said. "Can I try again?"

"Aye."

"Pirate Doug. Is that you?" she repeated, using his silly title.

"Aye, smelly sister it is," he replied, glancing quickly over at me to make sure he'd answered the question correctly.

I shook my head and giggled. He was an idiot, but he was my idiot and I was keeping him.

"Your brother is my mate," I shouted to the shocked Sea Hag. "This makes me your sister-in-law," I choked out on a gag.

"Yep," Madison took over, realizing I was about to hurl at the horrifying realization. "Which in turn makes you abstractly related to me, Ariel and Misty."

"And by association and suspension of disbelief, the rest of the hookers hiding on the beach with deodorant sticks," Misty announced, swallowing hard so she didn't lose her lunch. "Sea Creature Law twelve hundred and one point seven and a half states that family can't steal tourist property from each other without having outstanding hygiene."

"It does?" Doug asked.

The third time was always a charm. Janet decked her son's ass… again.

"So Bony Velma," I shouted. "What's your position now?"

The Sea Hag stared at her brother and he stared at her. The tension was thick and I wondered if my plan was going to backfire in a big bad way. Slowly, Bony Velma Dustface floated down to the beach with her Hags right behind her. We all took fighting stances and waited.

"You're his favorite," Bony Velma snapped, approaching her brother.

Thankfully Janet quickly produced a pile of clothespins and magically plugged our noses. However, she couldn't help our watering eyes.

"Pappy's an arse," Doug replied.

"So are you," Bony Velma said.

"Your point?" Doug inquired.

"No point. Just an observation. Pappy doesn't love me," Bony Velma stated and let her chin fall to her chest.

Doug considered the reeking woman for a long moment and then closed the distance between them. Wrapping his arms around her, he hugged her. We were going to have to soak him in tomato juice when this was over, but it was bizarrely beautiful.

"He has arse length green hair and a drinking problem," Doug explained to his sister. "I'm sure he loves you in his own fucked up way. At least he didn't pawn you off to the gods when he lost at charades—not that I mind being a Vampire. The regeneration benefits are outstanding. I'm embracing you with my seventeenth set of arms."

"No one loves me," she admitted sadly. "I don't have any friends,"

"And you thought terrorizing my mate and her people would remedy that situation?"

Bony Velma nodded and shrugged. "It was a long shot, but we thought we'd give it a try."

"Interesting," Doug said as he unsuccessfully tried to extricate himself from his sister's funky smelling arms.

"Why didn't you just ask?" I questioned, cutting in and trying to help Doug get out of his predicament. It was a no go. Velma's arms were a noxious vise.

"I don't know," Bony Velma admitted, pulling me into the pungent embrace with her brother. "We just wanted to be part of the fun."

"And killing my people would accomplish that?" I asked, realizing I too was going to have to spend some time in a vat of tomato juice.

"Well, when you put it like that it sounds like a shitty plan," Bony Velma muttered.

"Ya think?" I asked.

"How about this?" Doug suggested. "You let go of us before we pass out from your gamy aroma and then we come up with a real plan for you to be friends."

Bony Velma squeezed us tight before letting us fall to the ground with a thud. Everyone waited with bated breath to see what horrifying plan Doug would put forth—including me. I wasn't real sure how we could make peace with the Sea Hags, but anything would be better for business than killing each other on a daily basis.

"Oh shite," Janet shouted, pointing out to sea. "Kraken attack."

And then all Hell broke loose.

14

PIRATE DOUG

"FUCKING KRAKEN," I SNARLED. JUST WHEN I THOUGHT I WAS getting closer to getting jiggy with my Mermaid again, more shite hit the fan.

"That slimy bastard gutted our cave a month ago—killed about forty of my Hags," Bony Velma Dustface hissed as she moved and stood next to me. "What the heck happened to his skin?"

Wally, Tallulah, her sisters, my men and the Sea Hags joined ranks and we watched as the Kraken ate the remains of my favorite ship.

"My mother, Wally, electrocuted him," I explained, quite proud of the vicious woman who bore me.

"Your mother's name is *Wally*?" Bony Velma asked in confusion.

"It's Janet," my mother volunteered, holding out her hand to Bony Velma. "I knew your mother. Shabby Annie Slimecrinkle was aromatic … and unforgettable."

Bony Velma took Wally's hand tentatively in hers and shook it. Clearly my stinky, violent sister wasn't used to being treated like a normal person. If she bathed once a century and got some dentures, she might not have this issue, but I had bigger *issues* at the moment than my sibling's hygiene.

"The Kraken is after me," I said tersely, watching as the flaming pilfered furniture went down the greedy bastard's throat. "I'm apparently the heir to Pappy's throne and the nardhole doesn't like that."

"Will you have to dye your hair green?" Velma inquired with a wince.

"I'll be passing on the job if that's a requirement," I explained.

"Good thinking," she said with a nod of approval.

"Thank you."

"Krakens are impossible to kill," Tallulah said as her gorgeous lavender hair blew wildly around her head.

My Mermaid looked like an avenging goddess. Her ass kicking skills were outstanding. I wondered how she would feel about living on a ship and looting.

"By yourself it is," I agreed. "However, you are not alone."

"No time to get all Michael Jackson on us here," Bony Velma snapped as she began to emit an odor so noxious I almost fell to my knees.

"*What* in Poseidon's hairy ball sac are you doing?" I choked out. "Not really going to help if you kill everyone on the island."

"Krakens have a keen sense of smell," my sister shouted, signaling to the other Hags to let their funky stink flags fly. "It will disorient the fucker."

"And singe our noses off our bodies," Tallulah muttered on a gag.

"Not a problem," Wally shouted as she waved her hands and magically produced gas masks for us. "Stink it up, Hags."

"Will do," Rickety Shelia grunted, turning a deeper shade of puke green and laughing like a deranged maniac.

"I'm calling in the sharks," Tallulah announced as she went

to her knees and began to chant. "They can't kill the abomination, but they'll slow him down."

"Good plan," I said. "If we can confuse the slimy shite with my sister's rank BO and the sharks can take a few chunks out, I shall fly out there and behead it."

"But wait," Tallulah said. "It's kinda one huge head with some legs sticking out to start with. How are you going to behead a head?"

Her point was excellent and it gave me pause. How *did* one behead a head?

"Can't let the Kraken hit the shore," Wally yelled.

"Why not?" I demanded, still trying to figure out how to behead a damned head.

"If it hits dry land it will explode into thousands of little midget sized Krakens with sharp pointy teeth and frizzy hair. The tiny bastards will eat everything in sight—including us," Wally explained as she morphed into a massive version of herself. "I'll electrocute him, but that won't kill him either."

"Everything can die," I muttered as I paced the beach. I tried to think up a plan B or C or D or even Z. It was unacceptable to let the Kraken win.

"Bony Velma, do you have the Hag Daggers with you?" Tallulah asked.

"Yep," Bony Velma answered with a curt nod. "But they just piss him off. We tried that last month."

"Then how did you run him off?" I questioned as the Kraken finished off my ship and began to eye the shore.

"Not sure," she replied. "Might have been the aroma or the names we called him. Krakens have very sensitive hearing."

"How sensitive?" I demanded.

"Very sensitive," my sister said.

"How about this?" Ariel suggested, jumping up and down with excitement. "We get a huge tank of oxygen and shove it in the Kraken's mouth and then get a bazooka and shoot the tank.

But we might need Roy Scheider and Richard Dreyfuss for that. I mean we could do it, but they have more experience with it. You know?"

"Good one. Does anyone actually *know* Roy Scheider or Richard Dreyfuss?" I asked thinking it wasn't a bad plan.

"Oh my goddess," Tallulah grumbled. "We don't have time for that right now and that was from a freakin' movie, Ariel."

"The blue Mermaid might have a point," Bony Velma said. "Conventional ideas won't work. We gotta think outside of the box."

"He's getting closer," Wally hissed as she began to glow.

My mother sent out a shot of magic that lit the Kraken up like an electrified wire in a lightning storm, but it just shook it off and kept coming closer. The roar of the beast and the crashing of the waves did not bode well for an outcome in our favor.

Unacceptable.

"The sharks are here," Tallulah shouted.

Our finned allies stabbed and bit at the monster, but still to no avail.

Shite.

"We're armed and ready to go after the cargo thieving tar stain," Bonar yelled, brandishing his sword.

We had sharks, noxious body odor, electrocution, swords, and Hag Daggers. None of it stopped the ugly bastard. But wait...

"Hold your fire," I bellowed. I had something else up my puffy sleeve. As long as my sister was correct about the Kraken's hearing ability, it might just work.

"Wally, produce earplugs. NOW. On the count of three, all of you will plug your ears and fire all weapons simultaneously. Hags, get your stink on and throw your daggers. Wally, electrocute the beast. Tallulah, Ariel, Madison and Misty throw glitter fish bombs and keep 'em coming. Tallulah, direct the sharks to go for the Kraken's nards if they can find them in that blubbery mess. Bonar, Upton and Thornycraft, get your cutlasses ready. As soon as the fucker is in range, pierce the vicious monster."

"What are you going to do, Doug?" Bony Velma asked.

"*Pirate Doug*," I reminded her with an eye roll.

"My bad. *Pirate Doug*, what are you going to do?"

"Are you sure about the Kraken's hearing?" I asked.

"Quite sure."

I paused for effect while everyone waited for my answer. I just loved being the center of attention. "I'm going to sing," I replied as the eyes of my men grew wide with terror and Tallulah grinned from ear to ear.

"SHITE," Bonar screeched. "That'll blow the bastard to Kingdom Come."

"Exactly," I replied with a wide grin and a gallant bow. "On three! Wait... what should I sing? Any requests?"

"*Fifteen Men on a Dead Man's Chest?*" Bonar suggested.

"*Under the Sea* or *Part of Your World?*" Ariel chimed in.

"*Yo Ho Ho and a Bottle of Booze?*" Thornycraft added.

"Rum," I corrected him.

"Right. Rum. My bad."

"No worries," I told him. "Any others?"

"I'm partial to the Spice Girls," Wally said.

"I think a better choice would be *Yellow Submarine*," an unwelcome and familiar voice bellowed.

A magical wind laced with absurd power picked up and a flock seagulls shrieked and danced on the breeze. The infamous Clam Band dropped to the beach and began strumming *Hail to the Chief*. It was entirely *too extra* for me.

"Pappy," I said with an eye roll. "I have this covered. I don't need your help. Not to mention you're wasted."

"Your point?" Poseidon inquired, stumbling around the beach like a green-haired arse, as usual.

Before I could get out a witty and disrespectful response, Wally decked his ass but not before she'd kicked him soundly in the nuts. The God of the Sea was down for the count.

"Umm, Wally," I said, narrowing my eyes at my mother. "Was that really necessary?"

"You said you didn't need his disgusting, cheating, forever fornicating, drunk loser ass," she replied with a shrug and a smile.

"You did say that," Tallulah reminded me.

"Okay, fine," I conceded. "I said it—not exactly like Wally said it—but I'm not sure I really meant it. Even three sheets to the wind the obnoxious freak is pretty powerful. He might have been helpful."

"You don't need him, Doug," Tallulah said, looking at me with pride and adoration. "Your singing voice is so tremendously shitty and horrifying, you could probably take the Kraken on your own. But as Michael Jackson says... You are not alone. I will always stand with you. I love you."

"He said all that?" I asked, surprised.

"Umm... yes," Tallulah replied shaking her head and clearly trying not to laugh.

It delighted me that I made my wench so happy with my intellect.

"The swimming hooker is correct," Bony Velma said. "I will stand with you, the hookers and your masculine-ly named mother as well. Always. In fact, I'll host Sunday dinners in the cave from now on."

"Can you cook?" I inquired.

"No. Not at all," Bony Velma replied.

"Excellent. I shall have Upton teach you. I believe he cooks to your taste," I told her, recalling the pot of smelly arse he'd concocted for my wooing date with Tallulah.

"I stand with your sticky-fingered ass," Misty said, stepping forward. "However, if you ever hurt my sister, you will be singing soprano."

"I too stand with you, you pilfering, idiotic douchenozzle," Ariel said. "And I'll do Misty one better. If you hurt Tallulah, I'll rip off your sausage and feed it to the sharks."

"I agree with my sisters," Madison added. "But I'll castrate you and magically sew your Johnson to your forehead. It will be permanent and painful."

"Your sisters are harsh," I said to the Mermaid I loved.

"Yes, well, they love me," Tallulah said with a giggle. "And their plan is child's play compared to what I will do to you."

"Sounds good to me," I announced as I looked at Tallulah's family. "I can promise you on Poseidon's plastered posterior that I will treat your sister right. I love her violent and shapely backside—not to mention her excellent knockers—and I plan to make an honest wench out of her."

"Define honest," Misty said with a smirk.

"Incoming," Wally bellowed as the Kraken picked up speed. "It's now or never! Sing, boy. SING!"

And I did. It was outstanding or horrifying, depending on how one looked at it. I chose outstanding.

I suffered two rather bloody burst eardrums, but I was Pirate Doug, the most deadly and clearly tone deaf Vampire Pirate on the Seven Seas. I would heal.

However, The Kraken in its furious agony almost swallowed Bonar whole as my man went at him with his cutlass. Thankfully Bony Velma came to his rescue.

The Kraken did swallow my sister before it was done but promptly spat her out. Her stench came in handy. Who knew a Kraken had such a delicate palate?

As I warbled a medley of *Mary Had a Little Lamb, I'm a Little Tea Pot* and *Oops!... I Did it Again* by Brittany Spears, the beast began to tremble and quake. My army continued to fight and even the Clam Band jumped into the fray.

As I hit the highest note I could without castrating myself to reach a higher one, the Kraken exploded into millions of goopy albino pieces. The sound would have been deafening if I could have heard it, but luckily my singing had temporarily impaired my hearing skills.

All of my looted deck furniture flew through the air and landed on the beach. It was slightly charred from the Tiki torch debacle, but still quite useable. Everyone covered their heads as the contents of the Kraken's stomach rained down on the beach —everyone except me.

The bastard had eaten something very important to me— something that might guarantee the longevity of my Johnson.

Swatting away fish carcasses, several anchors, a flat screen television and a mid-sized automobile, I waited for my prize. There was a slight chance it was at the bottom of the ocean, which would suck arse, but I was a strong swimmer.

Or at least Thornycraft was. I'd send him down to retrieve it if the beast hadn't swallowed it.

"Doug," Tallulah yelled. "Watch out!"

I had no clue what she was talking about until it hit me square in the head. This, of course, hurt like a motherfucker, but I played it off so I wouldn't look like a weenie. It served me right to be concussed by the object. Getting nailed was karma because I'd stolen it in the first place.

"No worries," I grunted, hoping between the damage to my eardrums and head I hadn't lost brain cells. "It's safe."

"What's safe?" Tallulah asked as she sprinted over, tore off her sarong and tried to stem the blood flow from my head.

With an eye roll, I snapped my fingers and clothed my Mermaid. Her bits were not for ogling. Well, I could ogle them, but no one else could.

"I'm fine," I told her with a grin as I held out what was rightfully hers. "The fucker ate your treasure, but I got it back."

"You're my hero," she said with a giggle, wrapping her arms around me. "You're an idiot and I love you."

"I love you too," I said as I picked her up and swung her around. "How do you feel about living on a Pirate ship?"

"Umm, let's discuss that later. Okay?"

"Sure," I replied, making sure my arsehole crew was accounted for.

"This calls for a party," Bony Velma announced, wiping the Kraken guts from her face. "How about nine o'clock in the cave?"

"How about here?" Tallulah quickly volunteered. "We have more room and it smells a little nicer."

"Fine by me," Bony Velma agreed. "What should we bring? Appetizers? Dessert?"

"Nothing," Misty yelled and tried to hide her shudder. "Please don't bring anything. Ever."

"Alrighty," my sister said as she and her Hags took to the air. "We'll be back at nine."

"What should we do about him?" Tallulah asked, pointing at my passed out Pappy.

"Not to worry," Wally said with an evil little smirk. "I'll take care of Poseidon."

This did not bode well for Pappy, but he had it coming. I strode over to my mother and put my arms around her. "You are a heinous woman and I'm honored to be your spawn."

Wally's eyes filled with tears and she hugged me back, but not before she swatted the back of my head.

"You are my pride and joy. Most of the time you're an enormous embarrassment and I want to beat your arse, but I love you, Doug."

"Pirate Doug," I reminded her and successfully ducked her powerful left hook.

"Captain, do ye want us to clean up the guts and slime for the party?" Bonar inquired.

"Aye, mate. That would be fantastic."

"Shall we take a nap?" Tallulah inquired with a sexy little grin.

"If that's code for boink, I'm all in," I announced to the laughter of everyone on the beach.

Tallulah shook her head and sighed. "He's an ass, but he's my ass."

I'd not have it any other way.

EPILOGUE

TALLULAH

AFTER MANY HOURS OF RUM SHOTS AND KARAOKE, WE CAME TO AN agreement with the Sea Hags. Thankfully, Doug had opted out of the singing.

The war was over and we would now run a multi-island Bermuda Triangle tourist trap. After the human guests got incredibly soused on Doug's excellent rum, we would do a nighttime terror tour on one of Doug's many questionably acquired Pirate ships to the Sea Hag Cave.

The Hags planned to dance and act out scenes from the *Price is Right*. Bony Velma would play Bob Barker. Bonar had volunteered to man the ship for the excursions. Upton was keen on catering for the humans and Thornycraft wanted to juggle. This surprised everyone, but Thornycraft was full of surprises. His karaoke rendition of Air Supply's greatest hits was strangely moving.

Wally had magically whipped up a gross of clothespins for those humans brave enough, or drunk enough, to partake in the stinky adventure. It was a good compromise and everyone was happy.

Having our gold coins back meant we could make the

necessary improvements to the lodge and be back in business as soon as the stench of Hag was gone. Not to mention we could pay the Otherworld Defense Agency for a job well done —very well done. Things were finally looking up.

Of course, Doug had thrown a hissy fit when Wally and I informed him his pilfering days were over for the most part. If the idiot hadn't given me fourteen orgasms during our *nap*, I would have kicked his ass for being such a jackhole.

"Never again?" Doug whined.

Sighing dramatically, Wally shook her head. "You can still loot every other Tuesday, but only from criminals and corrupt politicians. That leaves you millions of people to steal from."

"Gnomes?" Doug asked.

"No," Wally and I yelled in unison.

After listening to Doug bitch for another hour, Wally morphed back into a parrot and crapped on his head. It took Wally threatening Doug that she would eat a vat of beans and then attach herself to his face that had my man finally agreeing to his new job. Wally's mothering skills were definitely disgusting, but she got the job done.

"So Pappy left?" Bony Velma inquired, looking a little better than she had earlier.

She stilled smell horrible, but I was fairly sure she'd brushed her hair and slapped on some lipstick.

"Aye," Doug said. "Left with an icepack on his nards. Said he'll be coming back to woo Wally once his pecker heals."

"That's going to be painfully interesting," Bony Velma said with a grunt of laughter.

"Aye, that it is," Doug said, grinning.

We'd informed the Otherworld Defense Agency of the success of the mission. Renee had been quite pleased. Apparently Doug's part of the deal was satisfied as well. Renee had used favors due her from the dreadful Gnomes to get them off of my mate's *arse*. A win-win for all involved.

My sisters were happy for me. They'd warmed up to Doug enough that I was certain they wouldn't castrate him in his sleep. I could also see they were now dreaming of their own dysfunctional happily ever afters. I expected they would be going off on their own adventures soon, but I knew they would always come back home. Maybe they'd even take a mission with the Otherworld Defense Agency...

"Doug," I whispered as I watched his crew of idiots hit on the very receptive hookers who were thankfully going back to their own islands later this evening. "What exactly are Bonar, Thornycraft and Upton?"

"They're arseholes," Doug said.

"No," I said with a giggle. "What kind of immortal creatures are they?"

Doug scratched his head for a moment and pursed his lips. "I have no idea," he admitted with a chuckle. "But they're definitely arseholes—the finest arseholes a Vampire Pirate could ask for."

I was tempted to ask the *arseholes* what they were, but decided that could wait for another day—or year—or century. I had a feeling the answer would be alarming. I'd had enough of alarming for today.

"So are you ready to mate?" Doug asked in a tone that made my girlie parts tingle.

"What do we have to do?" I asked.

"We just promise to love each other until the end of time," he whispered in my ear sending happy chills down my spine.

"That's all?" I asked, snuggling closer.

"That's all."

"No sex?" I asked, disappointed.

His laugh went all through me. If his mother and my sisters hadn't been present, I would have jumped his insanely sexy bones.

"There's definitely sex, Mermaid."

ROBYN PETERMAN

"Lots of sex?" I inquired running my hands all over his broad chest and beautifully muscled arms.

"Tons."

"I promise to love you until the end of time, Pirate," I said quickly, wanting to get to the sex part.

Picking me up and throwing me over his shoulder, Doug replied. "I promise to love you until the end of time too, Mermaid."

My squeal of laughter and the speed in which Doug made our hasty exit caused laughter and applause from our friends and family.

Life was so very good.

I had my sticky fingered Pirate and my happily ever after.

I also acquired a violent mother-in-law with a pooping problem, a funky smelling sister-in-law, and a father-in-law who was going to have bruised nards for the foreseeable future.

But most importantly, I had love.

Pirate Doug, with all of his faults, was perfect for me. And I was perfect for him. It wouldn't be easy, but easy's for weenies. We'd keep each other on our toes and we'd love each other until the end of time.

And the sex was awesome.

Life was indeed very good.

— The End (for now) —

NOTE FROM THE AUTHOR

If you enjoyed this ebook, please consider leaving a positive review or rating on the site where you purchased it. Reader reviews help my books continue to be valued by resellers and help new readers make decisions about reading them. You are the reason I write these stories and I sincerely appreciate each of you!

Many thanks for your support,
~ Robyn Peterman

Want to hear about my new releases?
Visit my website at www.robynpeterman.com and sign up for my newsletter.

EXCERPT: ARIEL'S ANTICS

SEA SHENANIGANS, BOOK 2

1

ARIEL

"Gather the swimming hookers," Pirate Doug bellowed, stomping through the lobby of the resort in his absurdly dated puffy shirt, knee high boots and breeches. "We've got a problem."

I rolled my eyes and tried not to laugh—or groan. He *was* a Pirate and he *was* five hundred years old... but come on, did he really have to dress like a Captain Hook wannabe?

"They are not *hookers*," my sister Tallulah hissed at her questionably intelligent but very hot—despite the bad fashion choices—mate. "We're Mermaids and if you can't remember that I'll twist your Johnson into a pretzel."

"Aye, my bad," Pirate Doug amended with a wide grin as he snapped his fingers and conjured up a steel pecker protector. "Gather the *Mermaid* hookers."

I giggled as I watched my sister's eyes narrow dangerously at her idiotic other half. He was every kind of ridiculous, but he loved Tallulah to distraction and she loved him right back. Training the dumbass to have social skills was taking up an inordinate amount of my sister's time. Which left running our

Bermuda Triangle island tourist business to me and my two other sisters—Misty and Madison.

I was getting bored. And if I was being honest... I was jealous. Not that I didn't want Tallulah to be happy. I did. I adored my sister. I just wanted to have my own adventures and find my true love too. And I certainly wasn't going to discover him stuck on Mystical Isle running a tourist trap for humans...

With an exasperated huff at her mate, Tallulah left the lobby and went back to work. However, Pirate Doug being the randy idiot that he was, copped a quick feel of her bottom as she exited. My sister's squeal of delight made me close my eyes and shake my head. I really didn't know what she saw in the dummy, but he clearly made her happy.

Me? He drove me nuts.

"Ariel, my lovely blue haired sister-in-law," Pirate Doug said as he swept grandly up to the front desk that I was manning. "Have you seen my arses?"

"Okay, first of all... gross. As far as I know you only have one ass and if you have more than one I really don't want to hear about it," I said with a slight gag.

"Not my arse on my backside," he explained. "As fabulous as it is, the world couldn't handle more than one. I'm talking about my *crew* of arses."

My lacking in the brains department brother-in-law was referring to his Pirate crew—Bonar, Upton and Thornycraft. And he was correct. They were *arses*. However, they'd grown on me in the six months they'd been living on the island. They were missing more brain cells than Pirate Doug but they were funny and bizarrely sweet. Understanding them was a slight challenge as they mostly spoke Pirate, but they'd become the brothers I'd never had and never really wanted.

"They're on the beach leading the human guests in Sunrise Yoga," I told him.

"Sweet Poseidon on a bender in a rum distillery," Pirate

Doug said, paling considerably. "That's a shite idea. Might be bad for business."

"Why?" I asked growing alarmed.

We'd just reopened our resort. After a drawn out war with the odiferous and toothless Sea Hags, we'd had a lot of rebuilding to do. Even though we now had a truce with the Hags, the damage had been done. We needed paying human guests if we were going to survive in the competitive tourist trap business.

"Upton is very flexible—can lick his own nards. Not sure that will be an appetizing sight before the morning meal."

"Are you fucking kidding?" I shouted, jumping out from behind the front desk and sprinting toward the colorful seashell encrusted archway that led to the beach.

"No, I'm fucking your sister," Pirate Doug replied in confusion, running right on my heels.

"No, I meant... never mind," I huffed. Trying to explain what one meant to Pirate Doug was a losing proposition that could take weeks or years. Most of us had simply given up.

I stopped short and sucked in a horrified breath as I came upon a terrifying sight. Upton could indeed lick his nards and was demonstrating proudly, much to the shock of the guests. He was twisted into a position that appeared incredibly painful. A few humans were snapping photos with their phones. We *really* didn't need Upton's face in his bits all over the internet. I was not of the mind that thought all publicity was good publicity. A Pirate with his lips touching his nards was *not* good publicity.

"Enough. Take your freakin' balls out of your mouth," I shouted. Never in my two hundred years on this Earth had I ever used those words together in a sentence. I covertly aimed a blast of magic directly at the object of Upton's tongue's affections.

Luckily the humans had turned their attention to me and

missed the sparkling blue spiral of magic that landed exactly where I sent it. It was a well-known fact that Mermaids and other immortal creatures were *gifted* in the enchantment department, but it was best that the mortals didn't actually witness all we could do.

"Me nards are on fire," Upton screamed as he sprinted his naked self across the pristine white sand and into the ocean to cool down his balls. "Ariel, yarr a blue haired, cod faced tar stain," he grunted right before he submerged his flaming testicles in the salty water. "Ye might be pretty to look at, but yarr an evil wench!"

The only part of his insult he'd gotten correct was my hair color and the fact that I was attractive. All Mermaids *aka* Sirens were beautiful. We were created by Poseidon to lure innocent men into our traps. That practice was now totally old school. These days the only traps we ran were for tourists and we dated immortal asshats, not innocent men—or at least I did.

A Mermaid's hair and eyes were set from birth. My color was blue, Tallulah's was lavender, Misty's was emerald green and Madison's was pink. Each Mermaid's hair and eyes matched and were unique to them. No two were alike. However, the color of our tails changed with our moods and our fashion choices. Later today when I had time to hit the water my tail would be shimmering black—I was feeling grumpy and Upton's disgusting contortionist act certainly didn't help.

"So sorry about that," I said to our guests with a smile plastered on my face that I prayed to Poseidon didn't look fake. "Please come back to the lodge. Breakfast is served—that is if you still have an appetite."

A shell-shocked looking group of mortals slowly made their way back to the festive outdoor restaurant at the resort. Upton, having realized he was soaking his injured nut sac in salt water continued to shriek like a girl. Thornycraft, Bonar and Pirate Doug were laughing.

I wasn't.

I *really* needed a vacation or an adventure... or at the very least, a day off.

Another day in paradise was sucking the big one.

"Upton did *what*?" Madison asked with her eyes squinted at me.

"Licked his own nuts in front of fourteen paying human guests. Two of them were children. I'm expecting a few lawsuits or at least some therapy bills," I replied, plopping down on the rainbow velvet couch in the luxurious quarters that I shared with my sisters. It was wildly colorful and eclectic —just like us. Tallulah had moved to her own lovely cottage on the other side of our island with Pirate Doug after they'd mated. This was a very good thing as they tended to be *loud*.

"Like put his *balls* in his *mouth*?" Misty inquired, trying not to laugh.

"Yep. And from where I was standing it looked like his nose was stuck in his crack," I replied with a shudder at the horrifying memory.

"Pirates are just all kinds of wrong," Misty said, shaking her head and sitting down next to me. "What are they?"

"What are who?" Madison asked as she snapped her fingers and conjured up three Pina Coladas. "These are virgin," she promised as she handed one to me and one to Misty. "Not that a porno exhibition on the beach at seven AM doesn't merit some rum, but I figured we can start getting soused at lunch."

"What exactly *are* Upton, Thornycraft and Bonar?" Misty repeated as she retrieved a bottle of rum from the stash we kept hidden under the couch. She topped off her own drink and handed me the bottle.

I took a healthy swig and winced. It was next to impossible for a Mermaid to get seriously drunk, but I was going to try. The day ahead was most certainly going to be filled with mind numbing surprises. Pirate Doug still wanted to have a *meeting*.

"According to our sticky fingered brother-in-law, they're *arses*," I said with a giggle as I took another swig.

"That's a given," Madison agreed and took the bottle from my hands. After chugging the remainder of the rum, she hiccupped and giggled. "But what kind of immortal species are they? I know they're older than dirt. I just don't have any clue what they are."

"Well, Pirate Doug is a Vampire and heir to Poseidon's throne. I know for sure the *arses* aren't Vamps," Madison said.

"How?" I asked.

"No sunscreen," she replied. "Ol' Dougie can't go outside without 100 SPF slathered all over him."

"Right," I said, trying to imagine which kind of creatures the idiots could be. "Well, most animals can lick their nards. You think they're some sort of shifter?"

"Possibly," Misty said. "But in the battle with the Kraken, none of them shifted."

"Hmm," I said. "Maybe their species is better left a mystery. There's only so much alarming news I can handle today."

"Speaking of alarming… does anyone have any idea what Pirate Slug wants to discuss?" Madison asked.

"Nope," I said, standing up and wanting to get it over with. "However, if the jackhole suggests we wear Hooter's uniforms again during work hours, I'll castrate him."

"Here," Misty said, clapping her hands and producing a dull butter knife.

"What is this for?" I asked, examining it.

"For *member* removal," she said with a naughty grin. "Our

brother-in-law can regenerate his limbs and *other* stuff. If you're gonna remove his Johnson, you're gonna make it hurt."

My grin spread wide across my lips.

I loved my sisters so much.

Having my own true love like Tallulah did would be awesome, but until that time came all my love and affection was reserved for my devilishly fabulous sisters.

Not exactly the perfect situation, but for now it was pretty damned good.

Visit www.robynpeterman.com for more info!

ROBYN'S BOOK LIST

(IN CORRECT READING ORDER)

HOT DAMNED SERIES
Fashionably Dead
Fashionably Dead Down Under
Hell on Heels
Fashionably Dead in Diapers
A Fashionably Dead Christmas
Fashionably Hotter Than Hell
Fashionably Dead and Wed
Fashionably Fanged
Fashionably Flawed
A Fashionably Dead Diary
Fashionably Forever After

SHIFT HAPPENS SERIES

Ready to Were
Some Were in Time
No Were To Run
Were Me Out

MAGIC AND MAYHEM SERIES
Switching Hour
Witch Glitch
A Witch in Time
Magically Delicious
A Tale of Two Witches
Three's A Charm

HANDCUFFS AND HAPPILY EVER AFTERS SERIES
How Hard Can it Be?
Size Matters
Cop a Feel

If after reading all the above you are still wanting more adventure and zany fun, read *Pirate Dave and His Randy Adventures,* the romance novel budding novelist Rena was helping wicked Evangeline write in *How Hard Can It Be?*

Warning: Pirate Dave Contains Romance Satire, Spoofing, and Pirates with Two Pork Swords.

ABOUT ROBYN PETERMAN

Robyn Peterman writes because the people inside her head won't leave her alone until she gives them life on paper.

Her addictions include laughing really hard with friends, shoes (the expensive kind), Target, Coke Zero Cherry with extra ice in a Styrofoam cup, bejeweled reading glasses, her kids, her super-hot hubby and collecting stray animals.

A former professional actress with Broadway, film and T.V. credits, she now lives in the South with her family and too many animals to count.

Writing gives her peace and makes her whole, plus having a job where you can work in your underpants works really well for her. You can leave Robyn a message via the Contact Page and she'll get back to you as soon as her bizarre life permits! She loves to hear from her fans!

Visit www.robynpeterman.com for more information.

Made in the USA
Lexington, KY
23 June 2018